THE RETURN OF LORD RIVENHALL

Amelia Rivenhall is delighted when Richard arrives to claim the title left vacant by the sudden death of her father eighteen months previously. But when William also turns up, claiming that Richard is an impostor and that he is the real Lord Rivenhall, her troubles are just beginning. She discovers that when a huge inheritance is at stake, impostors and rogues will try anything to claim their money . . .

FENELLA MILLER

THE RETURN OF LORD RIVENHALL

Complete and Unabridged

LINFORD
Leicester

First published in Great Britain in 2006

First Linford Edition
published 2007

British Library CIP Data

Miller, Fenella-Jane
    The return of Lord Rivenhall.—
    Large print ed.—
    Linford romance library
    1. Love stories
    2. Large type books
    I. Title
    823.9′2 [F]

    ISBN 978–1–84617–946–4

Published by
F. A. Thorpe (Publishing)
Anstey, Leicestershire

Set by Words & Graphics Ltd.
Anstey, Leicestershire
Printed and bound in Great Britain by
T. J. International Ltd., Padstow, Cornwall

This book is printed on acid-free paper

1

Lady Rivenhall sighed as she spoke to her daughter. 'How long do you intend to stand at the window, Amelia? The rain will not stop because you stare at it.'

'I am not staring at the rain, Mama; I am certain that I saw a carriage approaching. It is hidden now behind the stand of trees.'

'Nonsense, my dear; who could possibly be calling so early and without an invitation?'

Amelia finally turned; her green eyes alight with excitement. 'Exactly, Mama. Who indeed?'

Her mother joined her at the drawing-room window that overlooked the sweeping drive. To Lady Rivenhall's astonishment, and Amelia's delight, a smart carriage bowled into sight. The face of the many-caped driver handling the ribbons was muffled from their sight.

They both stepped smartly back from their vantage point, unwilling to be caught in such a vulgar act as peering from a window.

'It is, no doubt, a mistake. The visitor has lost his way and has driven to our door to ask for directions.'

'Whatever the reason, Mama, it will at least break the monotony. It must be six months since we had a caller of any sort.'

The Dowager Lady Rivenhall re-seated herself upon the sofa, nearest to the meagre fire, and smoothed down her green velvet skirts. 'I know it has been hard, my love, but your poor father's sudden death, last year, has left things so undecided. Until matters are clear it is better that we remain closeted here, and receive no visitors.'

'But it has been over a year now, Mama; how much longer will it be before the lawyers can find a male relative to take charge of the estate and release to us the funds to which we are entitled?'

'I do not know. It is a great pity your Papa did not stay in contact with his younger brother, your Uncle Edward. Heaven knows where he is now, or if he even lives. His profligate lifestyle, which caused the rift in the first place, may well have caused his death.'

Amelia almost stamped her foot with frustration. 'It is so unfair that we should be in this sorry state, unable to pay our bills, or the few staff we still have, when there is so much money sitting in the bank. It was typical of Papa not have the foresight to organise his affairs before killing himself.'

Lady Rivenhall was shocked. 'Please do not speak so, Amelia. Your father did not kill himself; he died in a riding accident, as you well know. How was he to anticipate that he would meet his maker at only two and fifty?'

Amelia was immediately contrite. 'I am sorry, Mama. It is just so frustrating, waiting for news.' But the news they were waiting for, at that moment, was the identity of the mystery visitor.

There was a discreet tap on the door and Foster, their antiquated butler, stepped in; his expression for once, almost animated. 'There is a gentleman below, my lady, desirous of speaking with you. I have taken the liberty of placing him in the library.'

Amelia jumped to her feet. 'I will come at once, Foster.'

'You cannot attend on your own, Amelia, it would not be seemly. You must have Martha with you.'

'Oh, very well, Mama.' She turned to Foster. 'Please ask Martha to come here immediately.' A few minutes later Martha, her mother's abigail, joined them in the drawing-room. 'We have a visitor, Martha, and you are to accompany me to the library,' Amelia told the middle-aged woman waiting for instructions. 'I will return here as soon as I have any information for you, Mama.'

4

Amelia, closely followed by Martha, hurried downstairs, eager to discover the identity of the stranger. Foster was waiting downstairs to announce her. The library, the only other room where a fire was still lit every day, was at least warmer than the cavernous, marble-tiled, entrance hall.

The butler opened the door and announced her. 'Miss Rivenhall.'

The tall, dark-haired man turned from his thoughtful contemplation of the fire. He bowed low. 'Good morning, Miss Rivenhall. Thank you for receiving me. I have brought some information from your lawyers, Metcalf and Metcalf. Perhaps you could oblige me with somewhere to change whilst you read them, for as you can see, I am somewhat damp.'

Amelia realized that he was, in fact, standing in an ever-growing pool of water. 'Good heavens, of course you are. I shall have you taken upstairs immediately. Martha, could you ring for Mrs Higgs?' The housekeeper, Mrs

Higgs, bustled in, all anxious enquiry. 'Good,' Amelia said, hiding a smile. The woman must have been waiting almost outside the door, in order to have arrived so quickly. She was not the only one enjoying the unexpected break from tedium. 'Could you show this gentleman to the Blue room? And please find him something suitable to wear whilst his own garments are being restored.'

The gentleman in question exuded good taste, and full pockets, from the cut of his dark blue, super-fine topcoat to the superb fit of his buff inexpressibles, and once-shiny black Hessians. He bowed again. 'Thank you, Miss Rivenhall, but that will not be necessary. My man, Peters, will bring up my boxes as soon as he has seen to the horses.'

Although rather surprised by this presumption Amelia returned his bow politely, with a nod of her head. 'Mrs Higgs, please direct Peters to the Blue room, when he appears.'

'Very well, Miss Amelia. Come this

way, sir, if you please.'

The man picked up the package of papers that he had placed on the mantle-shelf, and offered them to Amelia. 'I am sure that these, Miss Rivenhall, will explain my unexpected arrival here.' Automatically she reached out and took the proffered documents. 'I shall rejoin you soon. Then we must talk.' At this, the man strode after the departing housekeeper.

Amelia, her hand shaking, already suspected what she would find amongst the legal papers she had been given. Inside she found several certificates and a letter from the family lawyers, Metcalf and Metcalf.

The first document she looked at was a record of the marriage between Edward Rivenhall and a Miss Mary Marshal. The second, a birth certificate for Richard Edward Riven-hall; from the date she realized it made him almost eight and twenty. The third, and final, document was the death certificate for Edward, dated scarcely three years after his marriage.

Amelia barely glanced at the letter of introduction from the lawyers. At last their worries were over. There would be money to pay the bills and life could return to normal. The privations of the past eighteen months, which had so damaged her mother's delicate health, would soon be forgotten.

She gathered up the papers and rang the bell. Almost immediately the door opened, and Foster appeared, bristling with curiosity.

'Foster, please take these documents up to Lady Rivenhall.' She paused, enjoying for once the opportunity to have more information than the butler. 'Lord Rivenhall will be rejoining me here. I would like luncheon served at noon, in the small dining-room. Tell Cook that we would like soup, cold cuts, and the remainder of the game pie. Thank you, Foster, that will be all.' She turned to Martha beaming beside her. 'This is wonderful news, is it not,

Martha? You had better go to Lady Rivenhall for she will wish to come down to meet her nephew.'

The butler retreated clutching the papers and Amelia knew he would know their contents before her mother. His officious manner was a constant irritation to her, but his loyalty to the family could not be questioned. Martha, still smiling, hurried after him.

The sound of footsteps approaching heralded the imminent arrival of her new relative. Quickly Amelia sat down, not wishing to appear too eager. The door swung open and her glance was drawn to the man who appeared to fill the entrance. For a second their eyes locked, and something she did not understand passed between them.

He smiled and immediately looked less intimidating. His teeth gleamed white in his darkly tanned face. Remembering her manners, Amelia gestured to the large leather chesterfield opposite her position by the fire.

'Please be seated, my lord. We

obviously have a lot to discuss.'

The fact that this time they were alone, unchaperoned, appeared to have escaped the attention of both of them. Richard Rivenhall flicked aside the tail of his coat and sat down, relaxing instantly against the sofa, his long booted legs crossed casually at the ankles.

'Miss Rivenhall, you have obviously read my papers and must know that I am your cousin, Richard.' His voice was deep and attractive, his expression sincere.

'I did not know I had a Cousin Richard until now.'

'I realise all this must be a shock, but I hope it is a welcome one. Mr Metcalf explained how intolerable things have been for you. And I can only apologize for my tardy arrival.'

'We have managed, but I must admit that I am delighted you have come at last. My mother is not well and the worry has made her worse.'

'It is to be hoped that her health will

improve when the rooms are warmer and the pantry full.'

Amelia smiled. 'Indeed, I hope so. But now I am curious to know why it has taken you so long to get here. Where have you been all this time?'

'I was fighting in the Peninsula when your father died and had no reason to read obituaries. My mother had never told me that I could be heir to a title and a large estate.'

'I see, but, my lord . . . '

He interrupted her. 'Do you think we could dispense with formality and use our given names? After all we are cousins, are we not?'

This unexpected request caused Amelia to blush. Surely it was too soon for such intimacies? 'I am not sure it would be correct, my lord. We have only just met.'

'I intend to address you as Amelia; you must, of course, please yourself.' This statement was accompanied by a charming smile.

'Oh, very well then, I suppose I must

call you Cousin Richard,' she replied a trifle ungraciously. Then she smiled, feeling her reply had been rather churlish, and her face was transformed.

* * *

Up to that moment Richard had not realized quite how lovely his young cousin was. It was going to make his task so much easier.

'Now, let me continue. On my father's death my mother had sufficient funds of her own, to keep both of us. She reverted to her maiden name, and I grew up using the name of Marshal, and did not even know I was a Rivenhall.' He paused, his expression sad. 'My mother died when I was twelve and there was just enough money left to purchase me a set of colours, and so I joined the Army.'

'So young? You were still a child.'

'Not for long; the army is a place where you grow up fast, if you are to survive.'

Amelia could imagine how difficult it must have been for a young boy, recently orphaned, to make his way in the army. 'Please go on, Cousin Richard. Did you make good progress in your career?'

He nodded. 'Yes, moderate; when I resigned my commission last month I had reached the rank of major.'

Amelia was not surprised. She had sensed immediately that her cousin was a man used to command. 'I am impressed. But how did you finally discover you were the heir to Riven-hall?'

'Quite by chance; after Waterloo I returned to London and visited Blake and Sons, my mother's lawyers. I had been sending them my prize money, over the years, and they have been investing it for me. I needed to know how my affairs stood. I did not know, however, that they had been holding that pack of documents in safe keeping.

My mother had left instructions for them to be given to me when I reached my majority. They had no idea of their contents. Because I had not been to see them since my mother's death they had remained unopened.'

He leant forward; his dark eyes glittered in the firelight. 'I was astounded when I learnt that I was now a lord, and not only heir to vast estates but guardian to a cousin and responsible for an aunt. Naturally I came down here immediately. And I can only apologize again, for the unforgivable distress my absence has caused to yourself and Lady Rivenhall.'

The intensity of his gaze made Amelia uncomfortable. She rose, her butter-yellow muslin swirling around her slippers, in her agitation. 'Thank you for being so frank. I must go and speak to my mother; tell her all you have told me. Luncheon will be served at noon, in the small dining-room. Will you be joining us?'

He nodded, already on his feet. 'Of

course; I have sent for the estate manager however and shall be fully occupied until then.'

Amelia couldn't help thinking that the new Lord Rivenhall was taking over the estate rather more quickly than one might have expected. Outside Foster waited to speak with her. 'Yes, Foster?'

'Miss Rivenhall, Lady Rivenhall has asked me to tell you that she wishes to see you.'

'Thank you, Foster, I am on my way up. Lord Rivenhall is expecting Masters; show him into the study when he arrives.' Amelia walked briskly across the hall shivering as she did so. She stopped. 'Foster, could you have fires lit in here, and the dining-room?'

'Yes, Miss Rivenhall, I will have it seen to at once.'

Lady Rivenhall was waiting, desperate to discuss their good fortune. 'Come in, my dear. This is so exciting, is it not? After so long we will finally have things as they should be. What manner of man is he? Did you like him?

Sit down and tell me everything.'

Amelia sat beside her mother. 'He is a tall, dark-haired, dark complexioned man; not exactly handsome, for his features are too irregular for that. He has, of course, the Rivenhall eyes. He has a commanding presence and is certainly a man used to taking charge.'

'But did you like him, Millie? It is so important that we all get on; for he is now the head of the family after all.'

'It is too soon to be sure, Mama. But, yes, I think I do. He is charming and polite and his manners are easy. He is obviously a man of intelligence as well. He told me that he was a major, and he fought at Waterloo. Do you think he was a hero? I shall have to find out; for sure he will not tell us himself.'

Amelia collected the documents scattered across the side table. The introductory letter from the lawyers caught her attention. 'Good grief! This letter bears yesterday's date.'

Her mother looked up, puzzled. 'Does it? I had not noticed.'

'If it is dated yesterday, he must have driven through the night in order to arrive, as he did, this morning.'

Lady Rivenhall began to look uncertain. 'Perhaps he was very eager to take over his inheritance, Millie?'

'But why? After all we have been waiting for more than eighteen months; why should a few more hours matter?'

'I am sure I do not know, Amelia. And please do stop pacing around the room; you are making my head spin.'

Amelia paused in front of the window. The rain had stopped, at last. 'Luncheon will be at noon; you shall meet your nephew then. But now I am going for a ride, Mama. It will clear my head. There has been too much to think about this morning.'

'Very well, my love. But please take care; you know how I worry when you ride that huge horse of yours.'

'Sultan is a perfect gentleman and in spite of his size he would never dream of running off with me.' Amelia dropped a kiss on her mother's faded brown hair and headed upstairs to change into her habit. Maybe a good gallop across the park would clear her head, but would it remove the doubts she now had about Cousin Richard's story?

2

Sultan stamped his huge hoofs with increasing impatience. He wanted to leave the cobbled courtyard in front of his stable and gallop across the park. The head groom, indeed the only groom still working at Rivenhall, tossed Amelia into the saddle. She placed her booted foot securely into the single stirrup, adjusted her skirts and collected the reins.

'Now, Sultan, I am ready, so stop fidgeting and pay attention.' Amelia patted her horses' glossy chestnut neck, revelling in the corded muscles and barely leashed power she felt under her glove as she did so.

'Will I be going with you, Miss Amelia?'

'No, thank you, John. Poor old Molly would never keep up.'

'More's the pity, miss. If we still had . . .'

'Enough, John. Let us not repine on what has gone. Our fortunes have surely changed today. Lord Rivenhall is finally here and the stables will soon be full of decent horseflesh again.'

'His Lordship looked a flash cove, Miss Amelia, nothing shim-sham about him.'

Laughing at John's description of her newly acquired cousin, Amelia clattered out under the archway and down the drive, heading at a smart trot for the gate into the woods.

When she returned, an hour or so later, she had quite forgotten her doubts about her Cousin Richard. It was half an hour before noon; Amelia realized she would have to hurry if she was not to be late for luncheon.

The gong was sounding as she exited her chamber, dark hair smoothly coiled and re-gowned in her morning attire of butter-yellow muslin. Lady Rivenhall emerged from her boudoir, supported by her abigail.

'Mama, are you feeling unwell? Has

all the excitement been too much for you?'

'Please do not fuss, my love, I am a little fatigued, that is all. But I am determined to come down today to meet my nephew.' Martha stepped aside to allow Amelia to take her mother's arm and together they descended the elegant carved staircase.

Foster held open the dining-room door with a flourish. 'Lady, and Miss Rivenhall,' he said loudly.

Startled by this unexpected, and quite unnecessary, announcement Amelia put her foot through the hem of her mother's dress bringing them both to an undignified halt in the doorway.

'If you would stand still, please, Aunt Sophia, and let me untangle Amelia's foot from your train.' Richard smiled at Lady Rivenhall as he dropped smoothly to his heels at her feet. She found herself smiling back, instantly at ease.

'Good heavens, Richard, my dear boy, what a silly way to make an entrance.'

Amelia, in her frantic effort to remove her foot before Richard was obliged to help, had become even more entangled.

'Keep still, Amelia, you are making matters worse.' He was having difficulty containing his amusement as he grasped her trim ankle and deftly removed it. Amelia felt her face scorch. How could he laugh at her? He was obviously not a true gentleman or he would have treated her with more respect.

'There, cousin, you are free to move.' He straightened easily, shaking out the folds of his aunt's dress as he did so. 'Aunt Sophia, allow me to introduce myself. Richard Edward Rivenhall, at your service.' He stepped back half a pace and bowed his head in greeting, his dark blue eyes still alight with suppressed mirth.

'A bit late for such formality, Richard, but indeed, I am more than delighted to see you here. You have been sorely missed these past eighteen months.'

Richard's expression sobered instantly. 'For that, I apologize, Aunt Sophia; I will make every effort to restore things here, to the way they were before my uncle died, as speedily as possible.'

He offered his arm to Lady Rivenhall and led her, with every show of concern, to the table, where Foster was waiting to seat her. Amelia was left to make her own way wishing she could stamp hard on 'dear Richard's' Hessian boots. That her fastidious parent had failed to comment on the rent in her favourite gown demonstrated how taken in she was by his smooth words.

A cold collation had been placed on the sideboard in the small dining-room, hidden under silver domes. Foster, and their one remaining maid, Jenny, removed the lids with a flourish. Then Foster stood attentively waiting to serve.

'Thank you, Foster, that will do. We will serve ourselves.'

Foster bowed, and Jenny curtsied, at their new master, and quietly left the room. Amelia almost exploded with annoyance. How high-handed! He had only been here a moment and already he was ordering the staff.

Richard removed the plate from in front of Lady Rivenhall. 'What can I get you, Aunt Sophia? A little game pie, perhaps?' He glanced along the buffet. 'There is ham, and cold mutton also, if you prefer?'

'A little pie, if you please, Richard, and some of Cook's delicious tomato relish.'

Before Richard could offer his assistance to Amelia, she jumped up and marched across to join him. 'I can serve myself, thank you, Cousin. Although Foster and Jenny could have done so if you had not so summarily dismissed them.'

'I expect Richard wishes to converse in private with us, Millie dear.' Her mother's gentle remonstrance was enough. She turned to the tall, handsome man, standing watchful, only a few paces away.

'Please forgive me, Cousin Richard; it

is not my place to comment. You must order the staff as you see fit, of course.'

He inclined his head and smiled. 'There is no need to apologize, Amelia. You have had the management of the household for so long; I should have consulted you first. It is I who should apologize to you.'

Amelia tilted her head and looked directly at him for the first time. Reassured by what she saw, she half-smiled and harmony was temporarily restored. Plates filled, they returned to the table and this time it was Richard who seated Amelia.

Lady Rivenhall picked at her food. 'Richard, I am curious; Millie said you must have journeyed overnight to reach here so early this morning? Is that correct?'

Amelia's eyes were fixed on Richard, keen to hear his explanation.

'How observant of you, Amelia,' he replied dryly. 'Yes, Aunt Sophia, I did travel overnight. Do not forget I am, or should I say was, a soldier. The elements are nothing to me; neither is the dark. I saw no need to stop; after all you had both waited long enough.'

Amelia relaxed. She must not be so quick to judge her cousin in the future; what did she know of the harsh world of the military, after all? 'Thank you, Cousin Richard. A lesser man might have taken two days on the journey and we would still be eating in the cold, would we not, Mama?'

'Indeed we would, my love. I, for one, shall be eternally grateful to you, my dear Richard. So much has gone to rack and ruin here with no money to repair it.'

'Well, that time is past now, Aunt Sophia. Amelia, I would like to go through the household accounts with you this afternoon, if you are agreeable. I need to know what discrepancies there are and where repairs and refurbishments are required.'

Amelia looked at her mother for permission, unsure if being closeted unchaperoned with her cousin was acceptable. 'May I, Mama?'

'Martha can sit with you, then there can be no objection, I am sure.'

'Then in that case, Cousin Richard, I shall join you in the library after luncheon.'

Richard escorted his aunt back to her rooms and released her into Martha's capable hands. It was agreed that when the maid had settled her mistress for a nap she would join Amelia in the library.

'You are sure you will be able to manage without Martha all afternoon?'

'Yes, Millie, I shall sleep, most likely, the whole time. If I need anything I can ring, can I not?' Lady Rivenhall settled back in the white lace-edged pillows, her face almost lost amongst them. 'Richard is such a very charming young man and so well-looking, but so much bigger than his father. I think he must have made a formidable soldier.'

Amelia frowned. 'But he is dark, and has the same navy blue eyes as all the male Rivenhalls. He must have inherited his stature from the maternal side.'

'Indeed he must, my love, for neither your poor Papa, nor Uncle Edward, had his height or half his weight. Now, run along, Millie dear, I am too tired to talk and Richard will be waiting for you.'

Amelia hurried along the corridor; all the necessary papers and notebooks tucked firmly under one arm. She paused as she passed a gloomy portrait of a long defunct male Rivenhall. The face that stared morosely back had dark blue eyes and dark brown hair, like Cousin Richard, but the features were narrower and the nose less prominent, the brows less arched, and the shoulders, what could be seen of them under the starched white ruff, were quite definitely not as broad or well muscled.

She giggled, she knew which Lord Rivenhall she preferred, the one who had arrived so unexpectedly that morning. Pushing aside all worries about Richard's lack of Rivenhall features she ran lightly down the stairs and hurried towards the library. She was grateful Foster was not lurking in the hallway. His ridiculous formality at luncheon had almost overset her.

She stopped outside the door, to arrange her skirts and smooth her hair, but as always two errant tendrils escaped to fall over each ear. She supposed she ought to knock. Suddenly the door swung open, causing her to step back in surprise. Cousin Richard must have excellent hearing.

'Come in, Amelia, stop dithering about in the passageway.' Richard stood aside politely to allow her to enter. He grinned down at her. 'Surely you were not about to knock?'

She grinned back. 'Yes, I was, I am not sure what the correct etiquette is now. This is your house; we are your guests, not the other way round.'

'Do not be absurd, Millie. This is your home and it always will be. You do not need to knock on any door, or ask my permission before instructing the staff. Is that quite clear?'

Amelia was startled by his vehemence but delighted at his words. 'Thank you,

Cousin Richard. That will make things so much easier for Mama and me.'

The library had always been Amelia's favourite room. The leather volumes packed onto the ceiling high shelves had long been her inspiration and her solace. As an only child she had often been lonely but once able to read had found all the companionship she needed within the covers of the many books.

'Shall we sit by the fire, Amelia? I have placed two chairs and a table ready.'

It was only then that Amelia noticed Martha, knitting busily, in a high-backed chair facing away from the arrangement Richard indicated.

The afternoon sped by. Martha was dispatched to fetch freshly baked tea cakes which they ate, most inelegantly, as they worked. When the abigail was summoned to attend to Lady Rivenhall neither of them commented. By this time Amelia was so at ease in Richard's company she felt no need for a chaperone, whatever the accepted protocol. After all, she reasoned, as she watched Martha disappear, we are cousins; I am sure that these rules apply to strangers, not family members.

It was almost dark when she left to join her mother in her rooms.

'Well, Millie, have you completed your business with Richard at last? It is time to change for dinner. What can you have found to talk about for so long?'

'Cousin Richard is arranging to transfer vast funds to our account, Mama. We will never be in want again. Never have to scrape and save, and do without, or be at anyone's mercy. Is that not a wonderful gesture on his part?'

'Good heavens, Amelia, what a thing to say. It is not for either of us to comment on, or discuss, Richard's pecuniary arrangements.'

'Why ever not, Mama? And anyway it is he who discussed them with me. He wants us both to know that we will never have to suffer as we have these past months.'

Lady Rivenhall's pale green eyes widened at her words. 'What do you mean, Amelia? Why should we have to suffer; Richard is not unwell is he, he looks so very robust?'

Amelia realized that in her enthusiasm at the thought of being made financially independent and no longer obliged to defer to anyone for funds, she had misled her mother. She dropped her knees beside her.

'Oh no, there is nothing wrong with Cousin Richard. Just consider he drove through the night, in torrential rain, and he has had no sleep in four and twenty hours, but he is still as wide awake and active as I am.'

Lady Rivenhall smiled weakly. 'In which case, my love, why are you so agitated about being financially independent? Richard shall take care of you, and me, until you marry. Then, of course, your husband shall take care of you. So you, and any money you have, will then be his.'

Amelia sniffed in a most unladylike

fashion. 'In that case, I shall not marry. I shall remain a spinster and take care of you.'

'Thank you, Millie, how kind of you to offer. But what about when Richard takes a wife? You will not wish to be at her beck and call, surely?'

At the mention of Richard taking a wife her insides lurched unpleasantly. Amelia scrambled to her feet not wishing to continue the conversation. 'It is late, and I have to change. I think I will wear my new dinner gown tonight; it is a celebration after all.'

'What a good idea; I shall do the same. I do hope Cook is able to find something more palatable than last night's meal.'

'I have spoken to her. She is preparing a banquet; we will have several removes and a dessert. As soon as she knew she could replenish her cupboards and her staff, she was overjoyed. I believe that she sent John straight away to the village to bring back as many of our people as are still available, and as much food as he could procure.'

'Richard is going to be an excellent replacement for poor Papa. Do you think we will have the carriage again soon? I would so like to make morning calls once more.'

'I mentioned the lack of horses to him and he said he has it in hand. He also had the effrontery to suggest that I might give him Sultan when he has purchased me a more suitable mount.'

'And how did you reply, Millie, my love?'

'I told him if Sultan goes better for him than for me then he can have him.'

Lady Rivenhall chuckled. 'Capital, my dear. I shall come out myself to see him try; I lose count of how many times your horse carried poor Papa into the hedge before he accepted defeat.'

Amelia grinned at the memory. 'I must go to my room now or I will be late for dinner.'

'I shall come down in my own time, Millie, my love. Do not wait for me; I shall join you in the drawing-room, when I am ready.'

* * *

Amelia glided downstairs, radiant in a gown of emerald silk, with modest décolleté and short puffed sleeves. Her long gloves and pretty slippers were an exact match. She knew it was an unsuitable colour for someone her age, but when she had pointed out to her mother that it exactly matched her eyes Lady Rivenhall had not had the heart to refuse. The dress had been sewn from a length of Indian silk that Amelia had found in the attics a few weeks earlier.

Richard, half hidden in the shadow of the doorway, feasted on the vision floating towards him. If he had thought her lovely that morning, now he knew her to be truly beautiful. He was captivated. He scowled and turned his back; falling in love with Amelia Rivenhall was not part of his plan. At the light footfalls behind him he faced her, his expression bland, but his appreciation clearly apparent in his eyes.

'You look breathtaking, my dear, quite *ravisante*.' He stepped forward and took her hand, his touch burning through her thin silk gloves, and raised it to his lips. His eyes held hers and she found it hard to swallow.

'Good evening, Cousin Richard, and thank you. I am glad you like my gown. It is rather daring for someone of my age, but I love it.' Amelia twirled and her skirts flew out around her

Immediately the charged atmosphere was gone. The innocent delight in her new dress reminded him of her youth. She was not a sophisticated debutante, versed in the art of flirtation. He must take care he did not scare her.

Richard placed her hand on his arm and led her through to the dining-room. 'Would you like a glass of ratafia or orgeat, Amelia?'

She shook her head, her face screwed up in disgust. 'No, thank you, I dislike them both, they are far too sweet. I shall take wine with my meal, but nothing now, Cousin Richard, thank you.'

They heard the sound of voices on the stairs. Lady Rivenhall was on her way.

'Oh, Mama, what a lovely gown, I had forgotten you had that one in your wardrobe. The shade of burgundy is perfect for your colouring.'

'Thank you, my love. It is wonderful to have an occasion to wear it again.' She subsided, gratefully, into a chair, her silk skirts billowing around her like fiery cloud. 'I must declare, we make a fine trio, do we not, in our finery?'

Amelia allowed herself a peek at Richard, clad all in black, his intricately folded, snowy cravat, ornamented only by one large diamond and gold fob. He looked magnificent. Her stomach roiled unpleasantly as he returned the compliment. She looked away, feeling hot. Surely she was not sickening for influenza? She walked across and sat down gracefully, next to her mother, remembering in time, to twitch her half train aside.

Inside the spacious, well appointed room, the roaring fire, and heavy drapes, masked the sound of a second unexpected carriage arriving. Foster, ever alert, was the only one to hear the heavy knock on the door. Three heads, all dark, turned as one when he stepped into the drawing-room, expecting him to announce that dinner was served.

Foster cleared his throat importantly. 'A Lord Rivenhall has arrived and wishes to speak with you, my lady.'

3

'Oh dear, how can that be?' Lady Rivenhall said faintly and all colour left her face.

Richard took charge. 'Show the gentleman to the library, Foster. I shall be there directly.' His tone was clipped, his expression impassive.

'Mama, do not worry, I am sure there is a simple explanation. Cousin Richard will deal with it.'

Richard dropped to one knee beside his aunt and gently took her hands. 'Aunt Sophia, there is nothing to fret about. The lawyers have been contacting the remotest of male Rivenhalls. This must be one of them; he has obviously not been in recent contact with his advisors and does not yet know that I have been found.'

Lady Rivenhall rallied and a welcome pink returned to her cheeks. 'I am sure you must be right, dear Richard. But it was such a shock. Whatever possessed Foster to announce such a thing?'

Richard's face was grim. 'I have no idea but I aim to find out. Please excuse me Cousin, Aunt, I shall not be long.' He strode from the room and Amelia was glad she was not the man waiting in the library.

'Would you like me to call Martha, Mama?'

'No, my dear child, I am now restored. I hope Cook is able to hold dinner back without it spoiling. Do you think Richard will invite this person to stay?'

'I hope not, but if he has made a genuine mistake we can hardly cast him out into the night.'

Amelia stood up and began to pace the room, her doubts about Richard returning. It was a strange coincidence, indeed, that both claimants to the vacant title should arrive on the same day! Could Richard's night time travel now have a more sinister motive? No,

40

he was her cousin, she was certain of it. She could not wait a moment longer; she would see for herself what was happening.

'I am going to the library to find out. If this gentleman is to be accommodated it is I who must organise it.'

'If you must then I cannot prevent you. But I will have Martha with me; I do not wish to wait in here alone.'

Amelia gave the bell cord a hard tug and waited, tapping her foot, until Jenny appeared, hat askew, having run from the servants' quarters. 'Jenny, please fetch Martha to attend to her ladyship, she is feeling a little under the weather.'

The girl bobbed a curtsy and vanished, leaving the door ajar. Her footsteps retreating across the hall were clearly audible. In spite of her worry Amelia smiled. The young maid had a good heart but blundered around the house like an overeager puppy.

'It will be good to employ some more staff, Mama. Poor Jenny is not suited to her current position as parlour maid.'

'She is a good girl, Millie, and she tries hard to please. You would not dismiss her, would you?'

'No, of course not. She can resume her duties as Cook's assistant; she was far happier doing that.'

They didn't hear Martha's approach. Like all good servants she knew how to move silently.

'Martha, Lady Rivenhall wishes you to sit with her whilst I go to the library.'

Instructions given, Amelia kissed her mother on the brow, a token of love and reassurance, and hurried out. She had been chatelaine for the past eighteen months and it was her right, and her duty, to participate in anything that affected the estate and its occupants. Whether her authoritative cousin shared her view remained to be seen.

She hurried down the wide passage way towards the library. Even with the door fully closed she could hear an angry voice. Perhaps it was not such a good idea? Maybe Cousin Richard would not welcome her intrusion?

Undecided she hovered outside, hand poised to knock; the voice grew louder and the door was flung open and a tall, slim, extremely agitated young man erupted from the room.

His sudden appearance gave her no time to avoid a collision and with a flurry of bright green silk she was catapulted backwards to end in an ignominious heap on the floor.

'God's teeth, Amelia, what the devil are you doing out here?' Two strong hands encircled her waist and she was hoisted, unceremoniously, back to her feet. Richard grinned down at her, more amused than angry. 'Are you hurt?'

Amelia crossly shook her head, too stunned to object to his language. 'No, thank you, Cousin Richard; it is my pride only which has suffered.' She had temporarily forgotten the young man who had caused her downfall.

His obsequious apologies rudely jerked her attention from her cousin.

'My dear Miss Rivenhall, how can I apologize for my appalling clumsiness? I would rather die than harm a hair of my dear cousin's head.'

Amelia felt sure she had heard Richard murmur, 'That could easily be arranged.' under his breath, but when she glanced his way his face was all solicitude.

'I am perfectly all right, thank you. There is no need to apologize. How could you have known I was outside the door?' Amelia's words were smooth but her thoughts were turbulent. What an odious young man; and how dare he address her so familiarly?

'If I had been aware of your presence I would never have left the room so precipitously.'

Amelia looked over the fawning figure and her eyes inadvertently locked with Richard's. He raised an eyebrow and his mouth quivered at the corners. Amelia felt a fit of uncontrollable giggles bubbling up, but she knew it would be unforgivable to laugh. Even though his unnaturally high starched collar and violently striped waistcoat made him, in her eyes, a figure of fun.

Richard took pity on her. 'Allow me to introduce William Rivenhall to you, Cousin Amelia, he is a great-great-grand-nephew of your great-grandfather, or so I understand.' All this was said dead-pan, no trace of anything but urbanity in his tone.

Amelia inclined her head in greeting but was unable to speak. William Rivenhall bowed so low Amelia saw the pomade gleaming on his thin dark hair.

'I am delighted to meet you, Cousin Amelia. I hope I may take the liberty of calling you so? I know our connection must seem slight, but we are related and I am Lord Rivenhall.'

This last was stated firmly and Amelia no longer wished to laugh. How could he sound so certain, did he know something that she did not? 'I am pleased to meet you, Mr Rivenhall; but as I am sure you are now aware, Cousin Richard, my Uncle Edward's legal son, is now Lord Rivenhall.'

William stared, and Amelia saw with a shudder that his sycophancy was a front. This was no popinjay to be fobbed off. He was here to claim a fortune and a title, whatever it took to do it.

Richard stepped forward. 'I think we shall leave this discussion until the morning, Cousin Amelia. Aunt Sophia will be anxious at our prolonged absence.'

Amelia belatedly remembered why she had come to the library. 'Mr Rivenhall, I will have a room prepared for you. Do you have a valet to attend you?'

The calculating glint vanished from William's eyes and his fatuous expression returned. 'How kind, Cousin Amelia, but my man has already conveyed my bags upstairs. I believe I am to be in the master suite.' This astounding statement was greeted by total silence. Amelia was incensed and drew a steadying breath, ready to challenge this person's impertinence when a warning squeeze on her shoulder restrained her. She glanced up and Richard shook his head.

'Dinner is waiting, Mr Rivenhall, will you be long changing?' Richard enquired politely.

'If dinner is waiting, then I shall delay it no longer. I am sure, sir, that Lady Rivenhall, in the circumstances, will forgive my appearing in my dirt.' Before either Richard or Amelia could restrain him the unwanted guest dodged past and headed for the drawing-room.

'Oh no, Richard, he cannot be allowed to upset Mama, please stop him.' Richard reacted instantly and in two bounds had overtaken William and placed himself in front of the door. Only a fool would attempt to pass and whatever he might appear from his apparel, William Rivenhall was no fool.

Amelia sighed with relief believing the danger was over. They had both underestimated their opponent.

'Lady Rivenhall, I beg you, let me in. I wish only to explain why I am here.' For a slender man William's voice was surprisingly loud. Richard was non-plussed. Then like lightning he struck. The crash as his fist connected with William's chin left no doubt as to the efficacy of the blow. The young man collapsed without a sound.

Amelia was not certain if she was impressed, or scandalised, but Richard had silenced Rivenhall, and that was what mattered. He bent and gripped the unconscious man's cravat, preparing to heave him upright, hoping to remove him before Aunt Sophia emerged, alerted by the shout. Too late! The door swung open and Lady Rivenhall saw her nephew apparently murdering a young man who was the very image of her poor departed husband.

With a faint moan she clutched her heart and sank unconscious to the floor. Amelia stepped across the body to reach her mother. 'Mama, Mama, speak to me.' There was no answer. She took her mother's icy hands in hers and chafed them, hoping to restore some warmth.

Martha joined her on the floor. 'Best get her ladyship to bed, Miss Amelia, and send John for Dr Anderson.'

She looked around helplessly and saw William's upturned toes beside her. How could their celebration have turned into such a disaster?

★   ★   ★

'Let me take Aunt Sophia, Amelia.' Richard spoke softly, realising his young cousin was in shock. Too much had happened too quickly. He had seen the same blank stare on many a young soldier's face when he faced enemy fire for the first time. He knew to touch Amelia now might promote a violent reaction. 'Come, little one, stand up and let me carry your Mama to her room.'

★   ★   ★

From a distance Amelia heard a kind voice telling her to get up. Like an automaton she stood, swaying a little.

She watched Richard easily lift her mother and carry the limp body towards the stairs.

'Miss Amelia, are you coming?' Martha's sharp voice finally penetrated her daze and she stepped back into awful reality. At her feet was the inert, possibly dead, form of a man who called himself Lord Rivenhall, and on the stairs, in the arms of a second man who called himself Lord Rivenhall, was the unconscious form of her beloved mother.

Ignoring William she ran after her mother, calling to Foster as she did so. 'Foster, send John for Dr Anderson immediately.'

Foster, horrified at what his piece of mischief had created, was for once subdued. 'Yes, Miss Amelia, at once.' He pointed at the body sprawled on the floor. 'And this person?'

'Leave him there, Foster. Lord Rivenhall can deal with it, it is his affair.' Richard was leaving the room as she entered. Silently Amelia stepped round him and closed the door in his face.

Martha was efficiently undressing Lady Rivenhall and Amelia went to help. Between them they replaced the crumpled dinner gown with a crisp cotton night-rail, and then, whilst the abigail supported her, Amelia quickly removed the pins and feathers from her mother's hair before they lowered her on to a mass of soft feather pillows.

Amelia was worried. Her mother had fainted several times before, over-exertion or excitement could bring a spasm on, but always she had remained inert for a few moments only.

'Mama, Mama, can you hear me? Oh please, please, wake up.'

'Try the smelling salts, Miss Amelia, it sometimes does the trick,' Martha suggested.

Amelia unstopped a cut-glass flask and waved the pungent liquid back and forth beneath her mother's nostrils but to no avail. 'Her lips are so blue, Martha. I am so afraid her heart has finally given up. I will never forgive Richard, or Rivenhall, if she does not recover.'

'Now don't fret so, Miss Millie; Lady Rivenhall has had many a turn, and she always do recover. Don't give up hope; the doctor will be with us soon and he'll know what to do to restore her.'

'I do hope so, Martha. It would be too cruel to lose her now, just when our fortunes are improving.'

Amelia felt her throat tighten; she brushed unwanted tears away with her gloved hand. The dark wet stain looked ugly on the silk. Suddenly she hated the gown and needed to remove it.

'I am going to change. No, Martha, I can manage on my own, if you would just unhook the back for me before I go.'

Martha, who acted as dresser to both Amelia and her mother, efficiently obliged. 'Here, put this shawl round you, Miss. It won't do to go out like that.'

Impatiently Amelia threw the shawl

around her shoulders, covering the gaping back. 'Thank you, Martha; I will be only a few minutes.'

Back in her own chamber she stepped out of her dress, leaving it in a green silk puddle where it fell. The long gloves and slippers were discarded too. Amelia selected a simple, peach, dimity morning-gown with long fitted sleeves and high neck, from the rows hanging in her closet. She knew it had no back fastenings to delay her. She pushed her feet into soft kid shoes and she was ready.

She ran back along the corridor. There was no change in the patient. Lady Rivenhall's face was still as bleached and her breathing so shallow it was scarcely discernible.

★   ★   ★

Downstairs Richard had carried William to a guest room. He had his valet, Peters, transfer his own belongings from the blue room to the master suite.

After all, possession was well known to be a strong suit in any dispute over property.

'You had better undress this fellow, and make him comfortable, Peters. I will request that the doctor check him over when he has finished with Lady Rivenhall.'

Peters gave the recumbent form a cursory inspection. 'He'll be right as a trivet before then, my lord, don't worry. He's breathing easy and his colour's good.'

Richard shrugged, indifferent. 'Good. I suppose it would not do if he croaked at my hand, would it?'

Peters allowed himself a small smile. 'No my lord, it wouldn't. Leave him to me; I'll see he's all right.'

'Thank you, Peters. I shall be downstairs awaiting the doctor, if you should need me.' Richard closed the door quietly behind him. His new man, Peters, had been recommended to him by his lawyer when he returned from Waterloo and, so far, he had fulfilled every expectation. He was finding it strange to have a man-servant after so long living hand to mouth as a serving officer in Wellington's army.

Mrs Higgs, the housekeeper, was waiting in the hall. 'Cook wants to know what to do about dinner, my Lord.'

'Good God! I had forgotten all about it.' He noticed the housekeeper's recoil at his intemperate language. He must remember to moderate his words. Soldiers' manners would not do here. 'No-one will require dinner tonight. The staff can eat what has been prepared and what is left will do for luncheon tomorrow.'

'Very well, my lord, and thank you.'

Richard paced the black and white tiled floor. How far did the quack have to come? He stopped, remembering the village was a mile away, so providing the doctor had been at home when John called, the man should arrive any time.

The sound of carriage wheels on the stones outside confirmed his speculations. Not waiting for Foster he acted as doorman himself. The doctor rushed past him, bag in one hand and ran up the stairs, without speaking, obviously thinking the stranger in black was the butler. Dr Anderson was too concerned for his patient's health to indulge in idle chatter with a menial.

4

The elderly man drew Amelia to one side, his expression grave. 'I am sorry, my dear, but this time I fear there is nothing I can do.' Amelia could not answer. 'You understand what I am telling you child, nature will take its course.'

'My mother is going to die, yes, Doctor Anderson, I understand. How long . . . ?' She could not complete the question.

The doctor patted Amelia's shoulder. 'One day, perhaps two, maybe less but certainly no more.'

'Will she wake up?'

'It is possible, my dear, but I cannot promise. But she is in no pain; Lady Rivenhall's bodily systems are closing down gently; soon she will be in a better place and reunited with your dear father.' The doctor collected his bag and coat.

'Surely you are not leaving, Doctor

Anderson, not now? Mama might need you.'

'There is nothing I can do; it is in the hands of the Lord now, Miss Amelia. I will return tomorrow morning.' Amelia watched the stooped figure shrug into his coat and depart. How could he go when her darling mama was dying?

There was a slight noise from the bed and she spun round, terrified her mother had woken and heard the doctor's bleak pronouncement. But it was only Martha adjusting the pillows and talking softly to the mistress she had served loyally for so many years.

Amelia brushed the tears away and straightened her spine. She could pray for a miracle or pray for the strength to endure the inevitable. Quietly she returned to the bedside. 'Go and eat, Martha; I will sit with my mother. There is nothing either of us can do but watch and pray. I shall ring when I need you.'

Martha nodded and stood up clumsily, her knees were stiff after so long on the floor. 'Shall I bring you a tray, Miss Millie? you have not eaten since noon.'

Amelia was about to refuse, for she certainly had no appetite, then realized she would need all her strength to get through the next few days. 'Yes, that would be kind, thank you.' She paused; the visitors were also unfed. 'Could you ask Cook to send something in to Lord Rivenhall and Mr Rivenhall, as well?'

'Yes, miss; is there anything else I can get you?'

'No, you must get some rest if you can and return here at first light.'

The only sound in the bed chamber was that of the fire crackling merrily in the grate, casting welcome warmth into the room. Amelia moved a small chair to the bedside and sat down. There was no change in her mother's condition. She laid her head on the sheets and clasped her hands in prayer.

'Millie, darling, are you asleep?' The voice, little more than a whisper, wrenched her upright.

She stared into her mother's eyes,

hardly believing her prayer had been answered so swiftly. 'Mama, I was not asleep, I was praying and my prayer has been answered.'

Lady Rivenhall was too weak to raise her hand to her daughter's tear-stained face but she managed a gentle smile. 'Do not cry, my darling girl. You have to be strong. We both knew this day would come soon. It is time for me to go, my dear, to join your poor papa in eternal rest.'

'Please you must not say it, I do not want to lose you, I love you so much.'

'Hush child, I know you do, and I love you. You have been the best daughter a mother could have.' Lady Rivenhall was unable to continue as her life force slowly ebbed away. Amelia clutched her mother's icy hands and wept silently. 'You have Richard to take care of you now, my love, so let me go in peace.'

'How shall I manage without you to guide me? Cousin Richard is a stranger to me!' But she received no further answers. With a gentle sigh Lady Rivenhall gave up the ghost, leaving her daughter adrift in an ocean of unanswered questions and bitter recriminations.

Amelia's sobs alerted Martha when she returned bearing the promised tray. She placed it on the side table and hurried to the bedside. 'Oh, miss, not so soon! Oh my lady, oh dear me.' Martha's loud sobs were harsh in the silent room. For a few minutes they grieved for the person they had both loved above all else.

It was Amelia who recovered first. 'Martha, that will do. There are things that have to be done.'

The abigail sniffed and wiped her streaming eyes on her apron. 'Yes, miss. I'll be right in a moment.'

Amelia stood up and gently smoothed the sheets where her wet face had ruckled them. 'She looks so peaceful; all her pain and suffering over, she is with God now.'

'That she is, Miss Millie. And no one

deserves it more. She was a truly good lady, kind to everyone.' She was unable to continue and broke down once more, crying noisily into her apron.

Amelia watched helplessly, unable to offer any comfort. She was barely in control of herself. She knew there were things that had to be arranged, things that she didn't want to do herself, but could not recall any of them.

The soft tap on the door was ignored. Then an arm came round Amelia's shoulders and drew her away from the bed.

'Come, little one, there is nothing you can do here. Let Martha take care of things now.' Richard led her from the still figure in the bed and out into the corridor. There he lifted her up, as if she was a baby, and carried her swiftly downstairs towards the warmth and welcome of the library.

Behind him his valet, Peters, slipped into the bedchamber to organise the necessary rituals associated with a death. John had been dispatched to recall the doctor as a death certificate would have to be issued.

Richard shouldered his way into the library and strode across to the fire. There he gently deposited his silent burden onto a leather chesterfield. 'There, Millie, you will be better down here.' He handed her a small glass of brandy. 'Here, swallow this, it will warm you.'

Amelia refused to take the offered glass. The smell of strong spirit made her gag. Then the first of a series of violent shudders shook her slender form. Swearing under his breath at his inability to help in the accepted manner Richard made a decision. It was what he did best. He sat down beside Amelia and lifted her trembling body onto his lap and then enveloped her in the warmth of his battle hardened arms.

For a moment she resisted then melted against him and allowed her grief to overwhelm her, knowing she was safe from further harm. Knowing that Richard, although a virtual stranger, would, as her mother had promised, now take care of her.

Eventually she was done. With a final shiver she sat up and a clean white handkerchief was pushed into her hand. She blew her nose vigorously and wiped her eyes. Then she froze; her eyes flew up to meet Richard's quizzical stare.

She was sitting on a man's lap! The horror of the situation she found herself in was reflected on her face. Richard, recognising her distress at her unorthodox position, gently removed her from his knees and returned her to the safety of the sofa. He leant across to the mantle-shelf and pulled the bell strap.

Foster appeared instantly. 'Miss Rivenhall would like some tea. Has the doctor returned yet?'

'Yes, my Lord, he is upstairs now.'

'Good; have Cook put up some food for us and have it brought with the tea.'

'At once, my Lord.'

Amelia felt numb. She was finding it difficult to adjust to her constantly changing circumstances. Lord Rivenhall had returned and restored their fortunes, and a second Lord Rivenhall had appeared and then her beloved mother had died, and all in the space of the day. Her head drooped, her neck felt too fragile to support it. All she wanted to do was close her eyes, sink into welcome oblivion where sadness could not penetrate.

With a sigh she fell into a deep restorative sleep and was not aware of being carried back upstairs and placed tenderly on her own comfortable bed and neither did she remember being covered by a soft embroidered quilt.

★ ★ ★

It was full morning when Amelia opened her eyes. For a moment she felt well then she remembered and a black cloud of misery engulfed her. She turned to pull the cover back over her head then realized she was still dressed. She had no desire to get up, for what was awaiting her was too awful to deal with, but she could not remain in her soiled clothes. She heard the sound of her drapes being pulled back and bright autumn sunshine flooded her room.

'Good morning, Miss Rivenhall. Will you be ready for your bath now or after your hot chocolate?'

Amelia stared at the girl nervously bobbing a curtsy in front of her. Who was she? Where had this strange young woman appeared from? Too weary to question something of such unimportance she pulled herself upright before answering.

'Bath now, please. And take that away. I do not want it.'

'Yes, miss.' The girl almost ran from the room carrying the tray with the offending drink. Amelia heard the welcome sounds of her bath being filled next door.

The communicating door opened and Martha emerged in a cloud of steam. 'It's all ready, Miss Millie. A hot soak will do you good. Come on now, let me help you up.'

She allowed herself to be led towards the bath. Papa had installed the newfangled cast iron bath tubs, and water closets, upstairs the year before his death. She no longer considered them a luxury but a necessity, especially on a day like today.

After soaking in hot scented water and letting Martha wash her hair she began to feel more ready to face the day. When the water cooled and her skin started to shrivel Amelia knew it was time to get out and face the horror of a life without her beloved mama.

The black mourning dress, which had been made at her father's demise eighteen months before, was loose on her now. She asked Martha to dress her hair severely into a knot at the back of her head and then she felt ready to face what awaited her.

She found it difficult to walk past the door of her mother's chamber knowing she was no longer in it so she averted her eyes and forced herself on.

Downstairs she hesitated, not sure

which way to go or what she should be doing. Instinctively she headed for the library — it was warm and safe there. As she approached the door she could hear the sound of raised voices from inside. She froze; who could be so insensitive as to be shouting on the day after her mother's death?

Then she remembered the argument outside the drawing-room when Richard had struck the odious Mr Rivenhall and her mother, hearing the noise and seeing the fight, had collapsed.

A red hot rage consumed her. It was their fault her mother was dead. If Mr Rivenhall had not shouted and Richard had not struck him then her mother would still be alive. Without waiting to consider the correctness of her assumption she burst into the room.

Both men turned to fix her in their astonished stare. 'How dare you raise your voices in this house? Have you no sense of decency, no respect?' Amelia glared at them. Richard, instantly aware something was gravely wrong, stepped forward with a smile of welcome, but no words.

William, insensitive to atmosphere, continued his harangue, but now addressed it to Amelia. 'May I offer my sincere condolences on the sad passing of Lady Rivenhall, Cousin Amelia? I am glad you have come as I wish to offer my assistance at this difficult time. This man is an impostor! He is not Lord Rivenhall; he stole the papers and has come here to defraud you. You only have to look at him to see . . . '

'Silence!' Richard's icy command was instantly obeyed. William saw death staring back at him and sensibly retreated behind the highest, most solid, chair he could find. Richard continued, 'I must apologize, my dear, it was unforgivable and disrespectful of us.'

He moved smoothly to her side and, taking her elbow, turned her round and guided her back down the passageway. The less she saw of Mr Rivenhall the better.

Hardly knowing how she got there Amelia found herself seated in the small drawing-room. Richard rang the bell and another unfamiliar maid answered the call.

'Have tea and toast brought here, now, please.'

The girl retreated and Amelia roused enough to speak. 'Who is that girl? She is the second one I have not recognized this morning.'

'Mary is one of three new maids that arrived from the village last night. I know you should have interviewed them first, but Mrs Higgs vouched for their probity and I felt that was good enough. In the circumstances I felt you would not want to be involved.'

'Thank you, that was considerate. I am sure the girls will be good workers if Mrs Higgs has recommended them. Foster needs footmen, and John needs grooms now that you are re-staffing Rivenhall.'

'The matter is already in hand. I have also sent John to purchase a pair of carriage horses and a mount for you that he has heard about.' He didn't need to state why the carriage would be needed; they could hardly walk to the churchyard.

The tea tray arrived and Amelia found she was able to drink several cups but the toast was ignored. Richard frowned when he saw the plate of untouched food. 'You have to eat, Millie. Starving yourself will help no one. You will become unwell.'

She stared at him with dislike. The man was a brute, he hit people, took liberties with her person and was now accusing her of deliberately starving herself.

'I am not hungry. When I am, I will eat, not before.' She rose, her expression contemptuous. 'It is not your place to criticise me or tell me how to go on. You are little more than a stranger.'

'Hardly that, Amelia. I am your first cousin, and, I have to remind you, your legal guardian; I have every right to speak how I please in my own house.'

5

Amelia's eyes widened at his words. It was true; he was her guardian until she reached her majority. He did have every right to make demands that she would be expected to obey. Well, she could not prevent him taking over the estate but she would not answer to him; she would not be dictated to. Then suddenly it was too much and her defiance collapsed.

She nodded, sadly, too tired to argue further. 'You are correct, of course, my lord, and I beg you to forgive me. Now, please excuse me, I am feeling a little unwell and must retire to my room.'

Richard's expression softened. 'Do not run away, Millie, not from me. I can help you through this difficult time, if you will allow me to.'

Amelia hesitated. She really did not

wish to be alone just now. Richard stepped forward and took her cold hands in his. 'Look at me, Amelia,' he said quietly. Reluctantly she looked up. 'I am your friend, Millie, on your side. I will protect you, take care of you.'

He was very persuasive and Amelia allowed herself to be re-seated by the fire.

$\star \quad \star \quad \star$

But she would not eat the wretched toast however much he argued. Richard, seeing her rebellion, wisely refrained from mentioning the uneaten snack. He stood with his back to her, ostensibly warming his hands at the flames, allowing her time to become composed. A short while later he faced her, and with a friendly smile, he folded himself into an adjacent chair.

'Amelia, we have to talk. There are things we must settle. Are you feeling well enough?' She shrugged but made no reply. He took that as an affirmative. 'I have seen the vicar and the funeral is for the day after tomorrow, do you wish to attend?'

Stunned, she looked up. 'Of course, why should you suppose I should not wish to go?'

'It is not customary for ladies to attend funerals, did you not know that?'

She shook her head. 'No; my mother never mentioned to me that it was improper for us to see papa buried. It is a ridiculous rule; do ladies not have as much right to honour their loved ones, as gentlemen?'

Richard was pleased to see his deliberately contentious question had animated his cousin. He did not wish her to sink into apathy. 'Very well, my dear, you shall accompany me, if that is what you wish. I believe the custom developed to protect ladies from unnecessary unpleasantness.'

They sat in companionable silence for a while, both staring into the flames. Then Amelia recalled a problem. 'What about the odious Mr Rivenhall? Will he have to come?'

'Yes, I am afraid so. Although he is mistaken in his belief that he is Lord Rivenhall, he is still a distant relative of yours and will expect to attend.'

Quiet overtook the small drawing-room again. Richard watched the various expressions play across his lovely ward's face with growing apprehension. It was obvious she was not thinking about her mother, so she must be thinking about the events that had preceded her collapse.

Abruptly Amelia stood and began to walk around the room, her heavy black skirts swishing as she moved. She stopped in front of Richard and stared hard, as if trying to assess his honesty and worth. She came to a decision.

'Richard, there are several things about all this that worry me. But now is not the time to discuss them. I shall let the matter rest, but be certain, when this week is over, and I am myself, I shall insist on having the answers.'

He surged to his feet, towering over her, his bulk blocking out the warmth from the fire. His expression was impassive. 'Of course, Amelia, I completely understand. When you are ready to hear the answers you shall be given them. But for now shall we present a united front to the world?'

'Yes, that would be best. Nothing of this must be allowed to interfere with the funeral. Now, if you will excuse me, there are letters I must write, I am sure you understand.' Not waiting for his reply she walked away, head high, determined not to let her grief overwhelm her again.

★   ★   ★

The day of the funeral had dawned inappropriately bright. Amelia had hoped it would rain. But the late October sunshine bathed the park in light and the trees stood golden in their autumn finery.

She knew that Richard had organised everything to perfection. The funeral party, which would consist of herself and Richard, were going to travel in the Rivenhall carriage, pulled by the new black horses. The hateful William was to follow in his own chaise. The local gentry, who had been invited, would be waiting for them at the church. She was pleased that Richard had given the servants permission to attend and that they would be standing at the rear of the little Norman church to pay their respects.

His years of planning military campaigns in the Peninsula meant such a small event had posed him no difficulty at all. It was a relief that William Rivenhall had kept out of their way, keeping to the room he had been allocated, but now she would have to be polite to him.

Until today meals had been served on trays, in private; the curtains had remained closed in all the main reception rooms, as a mark of respect. Amelia wished that she could still be left to grieve in private.

The service was brief, the church freezing cold. Amelia stood numbly watching her mother's interment in the family tomb, glad that Richard stood by her side throughout the ordeal. Back at the house she nodded and thanked her guests but was unaware of their status or their names. The small gathering at the house passed with Amelia scarcely aware of what was happening. She had braced herself to endure the day without breaking down, but had only managed to do so by remaining aloof from the events and people.

★ ★ ★

Visitors thought her dignified and mature beyond her years, but Richard realized that the calm exterior was a façade that could crack at any moment. He believed he had come to know his cousin well over the last three days and to understand and appreciate her courage and intelligence.

He was sure when the questions came he would be able to put her mind at rest, but his first concern was to persuade her to eat before she suffered a serious collapse.

The butler showed the last mourners out and Rivenhall returned to mournful silence. The staff went about their duties sombre-faced, and Amelia, profoundly grateful she had survived the day without disgracing herself, retreated to the privacy of her room.

When Martha arrived with yet another, unwanted, tray she was resigned. Whatever she said to the contrary they would keep coming, relentlessly, until she gave in and ate something. 'What has Cook sent this time, Martha?'

'Soup, Miss Millie, and sweet rolls, nothing else.'

Amelia glanced, disinterested, at the offering, about to refuse. But the appetising smell that wafted from the tureen made her empty stomach gurgle. Maybe she should try a little, it did smell rather good. She sat down at the little table and dipped the spoon into the steaming broth, expecting her appetite to fail again. Almost of its own volition the spoon dipped and filled, dipped and filled, until to her surprise, and Martha's relief, the soup was gone. The rolls disappeared next, thickly spread with home-churned butter. Still hungry Amelia looked round for more to eat but the tray was empty.

'I expect you feel a lot better now, Miss Millie. We have been that worried about you, these last two days.'

Amelia smiled. 'Yes, I do feel better. However I think I will go to bed, sleep will bring an end to this dreadful day.'

★　★　★

Richard sat behind the substantial wooden desk, in the estate office, facing his accuser, William Rivenhall. He leant back in his chair and put his boots, insultingly, on the wooden surface. His posture was relaxed but his mind was alert and assessing how much damage the man could do to his reputation before the claim was settled. William eyed the boots with disfavour.

'Well, Rivenhall, let us begin. What is all this nonsense that you believe can expose me as an impostor and establish your claim?'

'You may sneer at me now, but I will find you out, and then the boot will be on the other foot.'

Richard smiled serenely, and pointedly, at his feet, resting casually on the top of the desk between them. William jumped up, goaded by this lack of respect, and, leaning forward, shouted:

'No, I shall not ask you these questions, or reveal what I know, I shall talk to Cousin Amelia; she will see I am the true heir.'

Like lightning Richard's hand shot out and his feet crashed to the floor. He grabbed William by the lapels of his fancy blue topcoat. His face was almost touching William's when he spoke. His voice was quiet, deadly quiet.

'If you go near Amelia with this, I shall kill you. She will be allowed to grieve in peace, is that clear?'

William, his breathing restricted by the vice-like grip, was able only to nod, which he did, vigorously. Richard released him and he staggered back gasping for breath.

'You are a mindless and uncouth soldier. You are not fit to be Lord Rivenhall. It will be over my dead body that you keep this title.'

Richard, his flash of temper gone, smiled, his eyes still glittering a warning. 'Do not tempt me, Rivenhall. I have spent all my adult life dealing out death without compunction.'

'I will not stay here to have my life threatened. I shall repair to the village. But as soon as Cousin Amelia is receiving visitors I shall be back and nothing you can do will stop me speaking to her.'

Richard stood up; he loomed over the slighter man menacingly. 'If you attempt to contact Amelia before I give you leave you will not live to regret it.'

★ ★ ★

William swallowed nervously. He was not going to win a trial of strength against this giant but he would prevail through cunning; in that area he had the upper hand.

He bowed stiffly. 'I shall bid you good day.' He did not call Richard by his usurped title.

Richard inclined his head. 'See yourself out, Rivenhall.' Then he turned his back and stared out of the window, apparently indifferent to the calculated insult he had delivered.

★   ★   ★

Furious, William slammed out of the office and hurried down the hallway to find his valet and organise his temporary departure from Rivenhall. He knew his claim was just and had no doubt that all this magnificence would soon be his. He was a patient man; he would wait and strike when his lawyers arrived. They had been making extensive enquiries and must have obtained some incriminating information by now. The impostor would not ridicule him then.

*　*　*

Amelia was descending the stairs as William, a new footman carrying his bags, departed. She realized that in the three days since Lady Rivenhall had been laid to rest, life had been continuing downstairs, as normal. The promised additions to the staff had been appointed, the house had been returned to its previous pristine cleanliness, and someone had arranged large vases of autumn flowers and placed them attractively on polished tables in the hall.

She was still sad, it would take much longer to recover from such a loss, but she was resigned and over the worst, and now believed she was strong enough to resume her duties. She had to meet the new people, take back control of the household.

She glanced round at the shining woodwork and sparkling windows and smiled. Richard was managing her responsibilities admirably but she felt sure he would be glad to relinquish the domestic details and get on with the serious business of running the vast estate.

She spotted Foster crossing the hall. 'Where shall I find his Lordship?'

'He is in the estate office, Miss Amelia. I am about to convey a tray of coffee to him. Is it your wish that I add a cup for you?'

She half-smiled, how pompous he had become since the arrival of Cousin Richard. 'Yes, do that, Foster.'

The office, a large sparsely furnished room hidden away in the warren of small rooms and passages at the back of the house, was where all the managerial work went on. In her father's time he had forbidden either her mother, or herself, to disturb him there. She hoped Richard was not so stiff in his ways.

Remembering how he had heard her

approach to the library, she tiptoed along the echoing uncarpeted corridor, not wishing to give him time to refuse to see her in his male domain. She knocked too loudly on the door and was not reassured by the barked response of, 'Come in, damn it!'

She flinched at his language and cautiously opened the door. Richard, dark head bent over a pile of papers, was scowling, not happy at what he saw there. Softly she advanced to stand, like a penitent schoolchild, in front of him. Nervously she cleared her throat.

'Richard?'

His head shot up and for the first time she saw him confused. Then his eyes lit and he smiled as he got his feet. 'Millie, you startled me. How are you? Let me see.' He came round the table cupped her chin in his large weatherbeaten hand, tilting her head to see her better. 'Yes, you are not so pale. You are thinner, are you eating properly?'

She laughed, immediately relaxed, for he sounded so like her mother, worrying over her health, that it was hard to remain standoffish. 'I am fully recovered, thank you Cousin Richard. And, yes, as I am sure Martha informed you, I am eating well.'

He dropped his hand and stepped back, still smiling. 'This is not a good place for us to talk, my dear, it is far too cold and untidy. Would you be more comfortable in the library? I am told it is your favourite room. Like me, you obviously love to read.'

'Oh, yes, I do. I am glad to hear you share my passion. Papa never cared to open a book unless it had stuffy facts and figures in it.'

As they settled more comfortably in front of the roaring fire in the book-lined room Amelia remembered Foster and the coffee tray. 'Foster will be looking for us. I suppose I had better ring and tell him where we are.'

'Serves him right! The man is an idiot.' An unexpected chuckle escaped Amelia's lips and she looked up, delighted to find a second point of agreement between them. When Foster finally arrived, red-faced and cross, they were forced to avoid each other's glance for fear of bursting into unseemly laughter.

6

Amelia replaced her empty cup on the tray and sat back feeling guilty that she had been laughing so soon after her mother's death.

Richard sensed her distress. 'Aunt Sophia would not wish you to be sad all the time, Millie. It is good to laugh a little, to lighten the spirits; it makes the grief easier to bear.'

Surprised that a man so ready to use violence to solve his problems could be so sensitive she answered without thinking. 'You are an enigma, Cousin Richard. You appear to be one thing then another, I am confused.'

'Then I think it is time we had our talk, do you agree?'

'Yes, I would like to. There are some things that are still puzzling me; may I ask you anything, without causing offence?'

'Of course. I want there to be no secrets between us. I already believe we are moving towards an understanding but it will not progress to true friendship until you trust me.'

The absolute sincerity in his deep voice rang a chord in her heart. How could she doubt this man? He had shown himself to be kind and helpful and she knew him to be brave and intelligent. She was now convinced that he was both honest and sincere as well.

Richard sat back at ease, his eyes smiling, waiting for her first question. 'Well, child, what do you want to ask me?'

'I am not a child, Richard; I am nineteen years of age. Although I suppose to a gentlemen as ancient as you, nineteen must seem positively childlike.' She accompanied this comment with an innocent smile.

'Good grief, Millie, how old do you think I am? I am a month past eight and twenty, not Methuselah.' Then he saw her face and knew she had been jesting. 'Baggage! Now are you going to ask me anything or are you not?'

'Not!' She rose and smiled down at his confusion. 'I have no questions. Your willingness to answer them makes them unnecessary. I am going for a ride; do you wish to accompany me?'

Shaking his head at her incomprehensible feminine logic, Richard laughed. 'I would love to accompany you. Shall we say that we meet in an hour, in the yard?'

'An hour?' She was perplexed. 'Do you have something urgent to attend to first?'

'Do I? No, you have to change into your habit.'

'Are you mad? I shall meet you at the stables in ten minutes, no longer, that is a promise.'

* * *

Richard watched his cousin run from the room, with a fond smile. He had been called ancient and mad by the same person in less than a minute and for some reason he did not mind one bit.

★ ★ ★

'Martha?' Amelia called as she rushed into her room. 'I have precisely six minutes to change into my riding habit.'

Six minutes to the second she was leaving her room in a dark green velvet habit, a matching feathered tricorn hat, perched jauntily on her head. She took the back stairs, it was far quicker, and moments later shot through the servants' quarters startling several new members of staff by her precipitous arrival.

Nine minutes after leaving the library Amelia strolled into the yard, a picture of loveliness, and revelled in the stunned expression on Richard's face.

John grinned at her. 'Morning miss; Sultan is raring to go; he has missed his morning gallops these last few days.'

Richard's face hardened. He stepped up and placed his hand on Amelia's arm. 'You are not riding that animal if he has not been exercised for three days.'

'Oh, bless you, my lord, he's been lunged every day for an hour or two; he's just not been ridden.' John nodded, pleased the new master felt as strongly as he did about the young mistress' safety. Richard released Amelia's arm.

'You must not worry, Richard, Sultan looks difficult but he is an angel with me.' The huge chestnut horse chose that moment to plunge and stamp, lifting the two grooms at his head clear off their feet.

Richard was horrified by this performance. 'I shall ride Sultan. You can ride the new mare that I have purchased for you. Is she still sound after her journey, John?'

The groom carefully hid his smile. 'Yes, my lord. She is fit as a flea. I will have her saddled and put your mount back.'

'No, you ride Prince; he needs the exercise. You can accompany us.'

Amelia could scarcely contain her glee. Richard was welcome to ride Sultan, but it would be a very short experience. Her stallion would tolerate no one on his back, apart from her. She wondered if she should warn him then decided that after his high-handed behaviour he deserved his comeuppance.

* * *

The side-saddle was removed from Sultan and replaced with one suitable for a man. The horse viewed it with dislike. He knew what would happen next. A huge human would thump onto his back and start yanking his mouth and kicking his sides. He snorted and stood ominously still.

* * *

The two conspirators exchanged worried glances, not sure their mischief was such a good idea. Richard took the horse's passivity as a good sign and smiled, looking forward to riding the handsome animal. He tossed Amelia into the saddle of a pretty grey mare inappropriately named Dolly, and watched John mount nimbly on Prince, and then it was his turn.

He gathered up the reins and allowed the groom to give him a leg-up; he just had time to stick his feet in the stirrups before Sultan exploded. Amelia and John watched helplessly as the horse did his best to crush Richard against the archway and scrape him off by galloping under the trees.

Richard could do nothing apart from grip harder than he had ever done in his life, and wrap the long mane around his hands and hang on for grim death. Sultan had the bit firmly between his teeth and not even a horseman as good as he could prise it out.

★   ★   ★

Amelia thundered after him praying what had seemed like a joke would not end in tragedy. She knew it was her fault. She had seen Sultan take hold of his bit; she should have told Richard before he mounted; now it was too late.

She had never seen her horse in such a fury. When her father had tried to master him he had just backed repeatedly into the thick prickly hedge until his lordship had admitted defeat.

Sultan disappeared over a massive hedge and into the valley below. Without hesitation Amelia followed never considering for a moment that her mount might not be up to it. She heard John landing safely behind her and galloped flat-out after the bolting chestnut.

Richard could hear the horses behind him and made another, ineffectual, effort to dislodge the bit. Sultan was deliberately slowing a little, he believed, and allowing the other horses to catch up.

'Sultan, Sultan, stop boy, stop!'

Amelia shouted, knowing that she was near enough for the stallion to hear her. He did hear her and stopped dead, pitching Richard over his head in a flurry of boots and flying coat-tails.

Dolly slithered to a halt and Amelia leapt down, not waiting for assistance, and ran towards the still form, face down in the mud. Was he dead? Was he hurt? She would never forgive herself if any harm had come to him.

She stopped beside Richard and his hand shot out and caught hold of her ankle, pulling her feet out from under her and landing her, with a thud, face first in the dirt. As she pushed her hands into the soft ground raising her mud covered face, a boot, placed firmly between her shoulders, pushed her gently flat again, and held her there.

'Next time you feel like playing a trick like that, young lady, think twice. It will not be my foot you feel on your back but my riding crop. Do I make myself clear?' She nodded; her mouth was too full of soil to speak. 'Excellent.

I believe that we understand each other.'

The boot was removed and she was yanked roughly to her feet. She stood, furious, filthy and spitting mud, in front of an equally enraged, equally muddy, but far more formidable, cousin.

Amelia raised her head, her mouth finally empty, and drew breath in order to express her views about someone who behaved as Lord Rivenhall had just done. Then she saw his countenance and wisely held her tongue.

John had exchanged the saddles and threw Amelia silently onto Sultan's back. The huge horse whickered a greeting and nuzzled her foot. His flanks were still heaving after his gallop across country and he was tired. But Richard knew the magnificent horse was not so tired he would not throw him again if he had the opportunity.

They returned to the stable in enmity; both Richard and Amelia too angry to speak, and John too scared. Sultan behaved as he always did with Amelia on board, like a gentleman.

★ ★ ★

Richard was too livid to appreciate the sight of the massive stallion bending his neck and trotting up to the bit for a rider a fraction of his weight.

He dropped to the cobbles and stood, arms folded, face grim, whilst John handed Amelia down. 'I shall see you in my study in half an hour,' he ordered, and then, still scowling, he marched off towards the house. His boots rang heavily on the flag-stones.

★ ★ ★

Amelia watched him go, not sure if her dominant emotion was fear or anger.

'I'd not worry, Miss Millie; I reckon he'd not hurt a hair on your head, not really.'

'He pushed me into the mud and stood on me; would you not call that hurting me, John?'

'No, miss, more showing you who's the master here. And we served him a poor turn, allowing him to mount when Sultan had the bit between his teeth. And he could have broke his neck when you called Sultan to stop like that.'

It was then Amelia realized why Richard had been so angry. 'He thought I called out wishing to unseat him? Oh dear, I shall have to explain I was trying to help him, not harm him.'

'Well, you'd best hurry and get cleaned up, miss, his lordship wants to see you in half an hour, don't he?'

Amelia gathered up her skirts and raced back to the house, taking the back door again, and ignoring the dropped jaws and wide eyes that followed her unladylike progress along the passage to the back stairs. She fled into her chamber praying her maid would be waiting for her.

'Good grief, Miss Amelia, did you take a tumble? Are you hurt?'

'I will explain later, Martha. I have less than half an hour to present myself in the study.'

Martha, although she had known Amelia since infancy, had the sense not to question further. No doubt Mrs. Higgs would know how her young mistress had become covered in mud. All gossip started in the kitchen.

Luckily, Lady Rivenhall, knowing her time on this world was limited, had stipulated that no black was to be worn for her after her funeral; therefore Amelia was able to choose a plain green, high-neck, long-sleeved gown. She had her hair plaited and arranged in an unflattering coronet around her head. By the time she was walking across the chequered floor of the hall, Amelia was no longer nervous. She believed, in spite of his barbaric behaviour, Cousin Richard was a fair man and would listen to her explanation and accept her apology, and the unfortunate incident could be forgotten.

The study door was open so she walked straight in. Richard, his stance uncompromising, stood facing the door and watched her approach, no sign of hesitation or fear in her proud carriage. He was, in spite of his anger, impressed.

Amelia halted a few steps from him and raised her head. What she saw sent her courage plummeting to her slippers. This interview was not going to be as she had anticipated.

'Cousin Richard, I must apologize . . .'

'Yes, you must,' he interrupted, 'but do not think a simple apology will suffice. I will not tolerate stupidity that endangers life.'

Amelia stepped back, stunned by the ferocity of his attack. Did he think he was on the parade ground disciplining a soldier? How dare he speak to her like that? A gentleman always accepted a lady's apology; she knew this to be true, because mama had told her so.

'I shall not be spoken to like this, Lord Rivenhall. I have apologized, which for a gentleman, should be enough.' At this point things might still have ended positively, but Amelia continued, 'And I can hardly be blamed if you are a poor horseman.' As the intemperate and unwise words flew from her lips Amelia wished them back. It was unforgivable to criticise his riding, only a first-rate horseman could have stayed on Sultan for so long.

She backed a further step, ready to flee if his temper broke. To her astonishment he laughed at her, but the sound was not reassuring.

'Well, child, now we know exactly how we stand, do we not? You think I am a brute and a poor horseman and I think you a spoilt brat, sorely in need of a spanking.'

She took another backward step, eyes wide, her face pale, and felt the welcome hardness of the door frame behind her. Without waiting to see what Richard's intentions were she spun and flung herself through the door and ran, pellmell, back upstairs where she slammed her bed-chamber door and locked it.

Breathing hard, and relieved she was alone, she paused, waiting for her heart to return to normal and straining to hear the sound of footsteps in pursuit. There were none. She was safe.

Unsteadily Amelia walked across the room, to sink onto the wide, well-padded window seat, a favourite hiding place of hers since she was a little girl. She sighed, ashamed of herself; she had fled from her accuser like a schoolchild. She was a woman grown, for had she not looked after her ailing mother and run the household, and the estate, without assistance? So why had she behaved with such immaturity?

Her obnoxious Cousin Richard had called her a child and she had undoubtedly proved him correct. She heard booted steps approaching her door and stiffened, but they passed by. Heart thudding, she resumed her pensive gaze across the rolling parkland.

A movement on the drive attracted her attention. A smart travelling carriage was bowling towards the house; it could only be the equally obnoxious William. She had had enough of cousins and counter-claims. Without their arrival her dear mother might still be alive today. Both Richard and William were the true culprits. Between them they had bought her nothing but misery and loss. It was their fault that she was a grieving orphan.

She scrambled up feeling calmer, no longer so lost and afraid. She would do her duty and run the house but from this moment on she would remain aloof from both her relatives. If there was a dispute, let the lawyers sort it out, she no longer had a preference, she disliked both of them equally.

She was well educated, spoke three languages, could dance, play and paint a pretty water-colour. Surely she could find herself a position as a companion or governess, and leave them to squabble in her absence? Lord Rivenhall and William Rivenhall were making her feel that the house she had grown up in was no longer her home.

7

Amelia dressed carefully for dinner, selecting a demure, but elegant, rose damask which emphasized her dark hair and pale oval face. As she had feared William was once more in residence and waiting, with Richard, in the drawing-room, for her arrival.

'Good evening, Cousin Amelia, I hope I find you well.' He stepped forward expecting her to offer her hand. She did not.

'Good evening, Mr. Rivenhall.' Amelia's voice was cold, her manner distant. She inclined her head a fraction and turned away to face Lord Rivenhall. 'Good evening, Lord Rivenhall. I trust I have not kept you waiting long?'

Richard's nostrils flared and his eyes narrowed. 'No, Miss Rivenhall, you have not.'

Foster appeared at the door to

announce dinner. Richard offered his arm, as was polite, but she ignored him, which was impolite, and stalked into the dining-room. The only person pleased by this display was William.

Amelia replied to direct questions from either man courteously but briefly. As Richard and William had nothing to say to each other, by the time the dessert was presented conversation had died.

'If you will excuse me, gentlemen, I shall leave you to your port. I have a slight megrim and am going to retire early this evening. Goodnight.'

Both men stood up, their chairs scraping noisily in the hostile silence, and bowed. Neither spoke. William, because he had nothing to say, Richard because he was too angry to trust himself to say anything polite.

Well satisfied by her performance at dinner Amelia glided upstairs. She would not have been so sanguine had she been privy to Richard's thoughts.

As the dining-room door closed

behind her he pushed his chair back savagely. 'Well, Rivenhall, when are your lawyers coming? The sooner we get this farce settled the better.'

William flinched. 'They will be here tomorrow. Do you have a legal person coming?'

Richard stared at William with dislike. 'No, of course not, why should I? It is not I who needs to prove anything, it is you. I have estate work to complete so I will bid you goodnight, Rivenhall.'

Richard, not waiting or wishing for a reply, strode off slamming the door with such force, that Foster, lurking outside, was forced to leap, in a manner not fitted to his dignity, to one side, to avoid being flattened against the wall.

* * *

Amelia took breakfast in her room, then as the weather was clement, decided to take Sultan for a gallop. On her return to the stable she saw a post chaise trundling down the drive. The lawyers had arrived. The issues would be settled and by the end of the day there might be a different Lord Rivenhall in Richard's place. Her stomach lurched unpleasantly and she blamed her breakfast.

Not sure if she would be required in the library by the lawyers Amelia took special pains with her appearance. The high-waisted, leaf-green, spotted damask emphasized her tall slender figure and set off her green eyes to perfection.

Determined not to allow herself to become confined to her rooms she swept downstairs as coffee was being taken into William and his lawyers. The small drawing-room was warm and welcoming. Amelia rang the bell and paced the Persian carpet waiting for someone to answer her summons. Finally Foster appeared.

'Foster, please ask Mrs. Higgs to attend me.' The housekeeper arrived, clean apron slightly crooked, minutes later. 'Come in and take a seat. We have much to discuss.' Amelia indicated the upright chair opposite her own. Mrs. Higgs subsided, her ample form in danger of overwhelming the chair. 'Do you have the menus for today?'

'Yes, Miss Amelia.' She rummaged in her commodious pocket and withdrew the menu and handed it across. 'As we have two extra guests I thought as you might wish for a formal dinner this evening, in the dining-room, so I have drawn up the menu to suit.'

Amelia glanced down the long list of suggestions, her heart sinking. If all this was to be served she would have to sit through an hour or more of intolerable tension. 'I think that it is too soon to be having anything as elaborate as this. We will dine, as usual, in the small dining-room. One remove only, and no dessert, cheese and fruit will be adequate.'

'Yes, Miss Amelia, of course. Will the gentlemen be wanting luncheon?'

'I have no idea. Foster must enquire. Please have a tray sent here, for me, at noon.'

'Very well, miss. Will that be all?' Amelia dismissed the housekeeper and collected the pile of correspondence, letters of condolence, which still needed answering, and carried them to a small table by the window.

She longed to know what was transpiring but her decision to distance herself from the dispute meant she could not ask. She ate a solitary lunch and returned to her work. At four o'clock the door opened and Richard strolled in. Amelia glared at the unsightly blots of ink that had appeared on her letter.

Richard half smiled at her agitation. 'Amelia, I have been looking for you. You are proving very elusive today.'

She stared blankly at him. What was he talking about? She had been in here all day writing letters, not flitting about the · countryside. 'As you can see, Cousin Richard, I have been busy in here, with my duties.'

Richard frowned. 'Then I was misinformed and I apologize.' That damned butler was taking too much upon himself. 'Leave that, Millie, and come and sit with me. I am sure you must be consumed with curiosity.'

It was as if no rift had appeared between them, no angry words been spoken. For a moment Amelia considered renewing the battle but her desire to know what had happened overcame her wish to prove a point.

She left her correspondence and took the seat indicated. Suddenly she wanted no animosity between them. Whatever he told her she wanted him to remain her friend. She smiled, all artifice gone. 'I am so sorry, Richard, I have . . . '

He stopped her. 'Enough, my dear, it is forgotten. As I hope my churlish behaviour is too? I have a bad temper and I am sorry if I frightened you. I would never hurt you, or let anyone else do so, I hope you believe that.'

Amelia did. She could not doubt him, his navy blue eyes shone with the sincerity of his words. 'Of course I do, Richard. And in future I will endeavour not to provoke you.' She paused and giggled. 'But I cannot promise; sometimes I cannot help myself.'

His roar of laughter echoed round the room and peace was restored between them. 'The lawyers will not be staying here, I am glad to say. They have caused enough trouble already,' Richard announced baldly.

'What has been decided? Richard tell me.'

He smiled grimly. 'What has been decided, my dear, is that although my documents are legal, they insist that the matter must be settled by my colonel, Lord Dewkesbury, coming here and confirming my identity.' His disgust at this arrangement was evident.

'Will that be soon?'

'I am afraid not, it will be several weeks at least, he is still with Wellington in Belgium. The letter will be sent, then we must wait until Lord Dewkesbury is free to travel.'

Amelia was worried. 'What about the estate? Who will be in charge until the matter is resolved?'

'The lawyers, and Rivenhall, have agreed that I should remain in charge. Unfortunately I can no longer transfer monies freely; all expenses must be ratified by the lawyers first.' He leant forward, his expression earnest. 'This means I will not be able to do as I promised; the trust fund for you cannot be finalized until my claim is proven. I am sorry, Amelia, I know how much this meant to you.'

'I have no need of the money, Richard. As long as the estate can be looked after and the staff paid, that is all that matters.' She laughed, remembering the decision made in the heat of her passion two days earlier. 'Do you know I had decided to leave Rivenhall and seek employment as a governess or companion?'

Richard stiffened and something she did not recognize flashed in his eyes. He grasped her hands in his. 'You must never leave Rivenhall, Amelia, it is your home. If anyone leaves, it shall be I, or

William, never you. Is that clear?'

Her hands felt warm and safe, hidden between his, and she was sorry when he released them and sat back. She found her voice. 'Yes, Richard, that is clear. I have no wish to leave here; I love it and cannot imagine there is anywhere else as lovely in the whole of England.'

There was a hesitant tap on the door and Richard immediately stood up. 'Enter,' he barked, not pleased his tête-à-tête had been interrupted. William came in, resplendent in multi-coloured silk waistcoat, green top coat and buff britches. He looked, Amelia felt, ridiculous but inexpressibly smug. Why should he look so pleased with himself? She glanced at Richard's impassive face but learnt nothing there. If he appeared indifferent to William's presence then so should she.

'I apologize, most humbly, for intruding, Cousin Amelia, but may I join you?'

She was tempted to refuse. 'Yes, of course, Mr. Rivenhall, come in. I was about to ring for refreshments, would you care to join us?'

William smiled. 'I would be delighted, thank you so much.' He sat awkwardly on the high-back chair, his ridiculously high collar making it difficult for him to turn his head. He brushed an imaginary speck of dust from his gleaming boots. 'It is a lovely afternoon, is it not, Cousin Amelia, and the weather is set fair across the country, I hear.'

Grinding her teeth, Amelia answered. 'Is it, Mr. Rivenhall, how interesting.' The refreshments were brought and consumed but the atmosphere remained strained. She did her best to maintain a flow of innocuous small talk but at all times she was aware of Richard's tension and knew that the smallest provocation from William would cause an explosion.

The effort was making her tired. 'If you will excuse me? I have a slight headache, and will rest in my room until dinner.'

They stood politely to allow her to

escape. She was relieved when she heard Richard follow her from the room seconds later and head for the estate office. Belatedly she understood that he had remained in the same room as William only to chaperone her. Touched by his concern she ran lightly upstairs, glad she still had someone who cared for her welfare.

★ ★ ★

So the pattern of her days unrolled, each day a little easier than the last, as she became reconciled to her loss. In the morning she rode out, and often Richard accompanied her on Prince. His disastrous ride on Sultan was never mentioned, although given time Amelia believed the horse would accept him. Richard had a natural rapport with horses and she noticed Sultan had begun to prick his ears and look round eagerly at the sound of his voice.

William had tried to ingratiate

himself with Amelia, but failed miserably. She had taken to praying fervently every night for the appearance of the Colonel, Lord Dewksbury, so that the tiresome young man could be sent packing. That it could be Richard who was sent packing was a notion she pushed firmly to the back of her mind. He was Lord Rivenhall, he had to be, because he had said so and he would not deceive her.

She might have forgotten about Colonel Dewkesbury if William had not constantly reminded her. Whenever Richard applied for funds to repair a cottage or purchase farm implements, William and his lawyers blocked the application. He insisted nothing but the minimum should be spent until the matter was settled.

Amelia believed Rivenhall itself would have returned to meagre meals and chilly rooms if it would not have adversely affected William's own well-being. He was a man who liked his creature comforts; that he also liked to drink heavily and gamble became more apparent as the weeks passed.

Amelia was forced to think the unthinkable. What if Richard was indeed the impostor William insisted he was? She carefully considered the evidence. William was the image of all the Rivenhalls depicted in the gallery. However Richard had the documents to prove he was who he said he was, and the family lawyers didn't doubt his claims; it was William's lawyers who, naturally enough, were disputing it.

She was glad that these black-garbed men had elected to put up in the village inn, and not reside at Rivenhall. Their daily visits were enough to bear.

* * *

The weeks slid by and the weather worsened, and Christmas was approaching, but no word from the colonel was forthcoming. William became more agitated while Richard remained calm, the epitome of a man with nothing more pressing to engage him than a lack of funds.

Amelia took her lead from Richard. She rode, sewed, painted and read. Sometimes with Richard at her side, but never with William. She began to listen, like Sultan, for the sound of his voice outside the door. She felt herself blessed by his company and basked in his marked attentions.

He never sat with her alone; Martha or Annie, one of the new parlour maids always sat with them. No proprieties were broken, nothing out of place was said, but Amelia believed that Richard was only waiting for his title to be confirmed before he made her an offer.

She was counting down the days to the time when he was free to speak. She realized she had been in love with her cousin from almost the moment she had seen him, dripping wet, on the morning of his arrival.

★　★　★

One morning, six weeks after the letter had been sent to Belgium, a reply finally came. It was addressed, strangely, to Amelia. With shaking fingers she removed the wafer and perused the contents. The note was brief.

Dear Miss Rivenhall,

I thank you for your cordial invitation to visit you at Rivenhall and regret the tardiness of my reply. Please expect me by the 15th.

Yours sincerely,
Henry Dewkesbury.

Amelia ran to the library to look at the calendar; it was the twelfth, so in three days everything would be decided. Thankfully Rivenhall had taken himself off to a pugilist event being held a few miles away and would be absent for two days.

Richard was, as had become his custom most mornings, working industriously in the estate office. Clutching the letter Amelia hurried to find him and tell him the good news. She knocked, but without waiting for his answer, burst in, waving the letter as she entered.

'Richard, we have heard at last. Your colonel will be here in three days. Is it not excellent news?'

Richard put down his pen and stood up. 'It is indeed, Millie. I am glad the wait is over and matters can be settled.'

'Should I send a message to Mr. Rivenhall, do you think?'

'There is no need. I am sure his lawyers will already have informed him.' He laughed dryly. 'You can be certain he will be here on the 15th. I have a few more things to complete so will you excuse me, my dear?'

Rather taken aback by his lack of enthusiasm, Amelia nodded. 'Of course, Richard, I shall leave you to get on. Shall I see you at luncheon?'

'I am afraid not. I have to go out directly and will not be back until dinner.'

'Then, I shall look forward to seeing you this evening.'

Richard nodded absently, and resumed his seat, his mind already on other things.

8

From her vantage point on the window seat Amelia saw Richard canter off down the drive an hour later. She wondered where he was going in such a hurry. She had decided to wear her emerald silk dinner gown; in spite of the unhappy circumstances of its last outing, she loved the way it made her look. Recently she had found herself more preoccupied with her appearance than she was used to, which had not gone unremarked by her dresser.

Richard returned from his mysterious trip, and, elegantly attired in formal black, was already in the small drawing-room when Amelia came down later. 'You look lovely, Millie, emerald is your colour.' He knew by now not to offer her a drink.

'Thank you, Richard.' She dipped her head in acknowledgement, glad they were, for once, to dine without their unwelcome guest. But dinner was not the happy meal she had hoped. Richard was abstracted and not inclined to talk. Exasperated by his inattention she finally put politeness to one side and said what was on her mind.

'Cousin Richard, what is wrong? You have scarcely said three words to me in the past twenty minutes. Have I done something to offend you?'

He reached out and captured her waving hand. 'I have much to think about, my dear. I must apologize if I have been neglecting you.'

The butler returned to clear the covers and instantly Richard released her. When the servants had left he pushed his chair back angrily.

'This is no good. I have to talk to you without these interruptions. Will you agree to meet me in the library later tonight, when everyone is in bed and we may have privacy?'

Amelia's spirits soared. He was going to declare his intentions. So that was why he had been so preoccupied. 'Yes, of course I will. I shall retire now, but what time shall I rejoin you?'

'11 o'clock — even Foster should be abed by then.' Richard came round and pulled her chair out for her, his hands brushing her bare shoulders as he did so. His gentle touch sent a frisson of excitement rippling through her.

'Until later then, Richard, goodnight.'

'Goodnight, Millie, I shall be waiting.'

Amelia floated upstairs, her head full of plans for the new life she would have as Lady Rivenhall. She understood that it would have to be a small wedding; it was too soon since her dear mother had gone to join papa in eternal rest.

She had been dreading the Christmas celebration without her mother. Now she had something to look forward to. She wondered if Richard would want to take a wedding trip; she had never ventured further than the nearby market town and the idea of seeing more of the world was exciting.

If Martha was surprised to see her back so early, and so happy, she was too well trained to comment. 'Will you be needing me again tonight, Miss Millie?' She asked this as she hung the silk dress back in the closet.

'No, Martha, you may go. I intend to read before I sleep, so leave the lamps burning if you please.' Her maid departed through the servant's door in the dressing-room leaving Amelia with her thoughts. She had almost one and a half hours to wait before her exciting assignation and the time refused to pass.

At last it was time to go; she tied her dressing-gown more firmly and then placed a pretty cashmere wrap around her. It would be cold downstairs now the fires were out. She crept to the door and silently opened it a crack. The corridor outside was inky black.

Like a wraith, her unbound hair floating around her shoulders, she left her bedchamber. Candlestick aloft in one hand, her skirts held in the other, she slipped down the stairway, tiptoeing across the echoing hall and into the passageway that led to the library.

The door was ajar and she could see the flicker of fire and candlelight within. Richard was there before her. The fact that meeting a man, unchaperoned, in her nightgown, would hopelessly compromise her if ever it became known had not even occurred to her. If it had she would still have gone. She was meeting Richard, the man she loved, the man whom she was going to marry; he would never have suggested anything that might harm her reputation or her person.

'Come in, Millie, and close the door, I do not want us to be disturbed.' Richard spoke softly from his position by the fire, but made no move to meet her.

Amelia giggled. 'This is so exciting, Richard. It is years since I stole about Rivenhall in the dark.'

He didn't return her smile. In fact he looked serious, unlike the man she had come to know so well. 'Sit down, on the sofa, Millie, there is much I have to tell you, and none of it will make pleasant hearing.'

She sat, her pulse fluttering unpleasantly. What he did next finally made her recognize how stupid she had been to agree to this meeting. He strode across to the door, turned the key, removed it, and placed it in the pocket of his brocade dressing gown.

Her eyes were huge and all colour left her face. When he saw her fear Richard used words she had never heard before.

'I am sorry, sweetheart, but I can not have you bolting before I finish. I give you my word of honour, I shall not harm you. Do you understand?' She nodded, unable to speak. 'Good girl. Please promise not to interrupt; you will have plenty of time for questions at the end.'

Again she nodded, sick to her stomach, for there was only one thing Richard could tell her that would make her run away. That he was not, after all, the real Lord Rivenhall. How could he have lied to her? Deceived her so cruelly?

★   ★   ★

Richard watched as the knowledge of his perfidy was reflected on her face. She had guessed. Good — now he could begin his story. 'I am not Lord Rivenhall, I believe you have just worked that out, but I am not a black-hearted villain, whatever it might seem. I must tell you my story and hope you can understand, and forgive me for what I have done. My story starts at Waterloo.'

★   ★   ★

Major Richard Marshall lay mortally wounded; a French sabre-slash had done for him. He knew he had at best a few hours, but would that be time enough to organize things, to convince his dearest and closest friend, Captain

Richard Jones, to do what he wanted?

'Dickon, there is nothing you can do my friend. It is all over. I am done for, we both know that.'

Captain Richard Jones, better known to his friends as Dickon, knelt beside the dying man. His bloodstained face and fierce demeanour made him seem demonic in the flickering light of their single candle.

'I know that, Richard, but at least we are together. We always said we would die, as we have lived, side-by-side.' Grief etched thick lines on either side of his mouth. He had spent the last ten years as second-in-command, to this man, who was all the family he possessed. And now he was to lose him.

'There is something you can do for me. It is my dying wish. Will you give me your solemn vow that you will honour my request?'

Without hesitation Dickon answered. 'I swear I shall do it, or die in the attempt.'

Richard shifted, a slight groan escaping his lips; his narrow features contorted, and he gripped his friend's hand. 'Thank you, I would do the same for you, if our positions were reversed.'

He gestured weakly to his saddlebags thrown carelessly on the floor with his saddle when Dickon had carried him from the battlefield. This half-burnt cottage was ideal to shelter in. The sound of musket and rifle fire, heavy cannon and screaming men and horses could be heard all around them. But here, Richard felt, it was peaceful, perfect for his purpose and as good a place as any to die.

'Look inside, quickly, we do not have much time.' Captain Jones opened the bag and extracted a letter several pages thick. Even on his deathbed Richard Marshall expected to be obeyed. His friend held each page before the feeble flame and read, to his astonishment, that plain Major Marshall was really Richard Edward Rivenhall, a peer of the realm, and inheritor of vast estates in Hampshire.

'Good God, Richard, you are a nob!

How come you never mentioned it?'

'I did not know myself until two weeks ago. My father was estranged from his brother and he died long before my uncle, Lord Rivenhall. My mother's brief marriage had not been happy so when she was widowed she reverted to her maiden name. She had enough money to support us in reasonable comfort and to pay for my education. I always wanted to join the army so when my mother died I bought my colours and began my career.' He coughed, and pink spittle trickled from his lips. Dickon wiped it away, with a sinking heart, knowing his dearest friend was soon to depart this life and leave him with some impossible task to fulfill.

Richard rallied a little. 'It appears that the lawyers have been searching for a legitimate heir for months. Eventually they discovered my existence and sent me the letter you have in your hand.' He stopped, too exhausted to continue.

Dickon watched his friend struggle to

find the strength to continue. Eventually he spoke again, but his voice was little more than a whisper.

'I want you to become Lord Rivenhall, take on my persona. We have, after all, often been mistaken for brothers. We are the same age and height, we have similar complexions and our hair is dark brown. Good God, we even have the same strange coloured eyes. The only difference is in our build, as you are twice my weight.'

'But I know nothing about your family, or ancestral home. I would be uncovered as an impostor at once.'

'No, that is why it will work. I did not even know I was a Rivenhall until last month. I know nothing of my father's family, so no one will expect you to either. We have spent the last ten years together. You know more about me, and my habits, than anyone else in the world.'

Dickon sat back on his heels. What Richard said made sense. 'I shall have to go to see your lawyers, the ones who sent you the letter; surely they will know that I am not you?'

'I have never seen any of them. Why should I have done? My own lawyers, Blake and Sons, who have been investing my bounty, have not seen me since I was a stripling. You are enough like me to cause no worries. I shall give you my letter, all you have to do is present yourself to Blake first, and then to Metcalf, as Richard Rivenhall, the rest will follow.'

Talking had weakened him further and his eyelids fluttered closed, but he still breathed, he was sleeping. God knows, Dickon thought, we are all exhausted; no one has slept for days. Whilst his friend slept fitfully he sat and considered what he had been told and reread the letter. What had been suggested seemed possible but why did his friend wish him to become Lord Rivenhall? Was he trying to help him up a rung in society, give him his estates in return for years of comradeship? Richard stirred and opened his eyes.

'I could do this Richard, but not until I know why. I have no wish to be a lord. I have more than enough money invested in the funds to buy an estate in the country and live a comfortable life as a gentleman.'

Richard smiled. 'There is a cousin, Amelia, she will be nineteen or thereabouts, and an aunt, not in the best of health; it is all there in the letter, you must read it more closely later. I am the true, direct heir; I do not wish the title, or the estate, to fall into the hands of some distant, remote connection.' Dickon was about to interrupt, say that sending him, an unrelated stranger, would be even worse, but his friend shook his head slightly.

'I want Rivenhall managed properly, its people cared for, and I know you will do that. No one could do it better. Also I want you to marry Amelia; then your children will be true Rivenhalls through the distaff side.'

Dickon was about to protest but

Richard gripped his hand fiercely.

'You swore, you gave me your word you would do this. I want to die knowing I have secured my title and my estates. Promise me you will do it.'

He had no choice. 'I promise, Richard, I shall keep my oath.' The hand holding his went slack and his friend was gone, leaving him with a double burden; his grief and an impossible task.

With extreme distaste he removed the epaulettes from his friend's jacket and replaced his Captain's insignia with those of a major. The first easy part of the deception was accomplished. Next he buried his friend and taking up the discarded saddle left the cottage. The battle sounds had faded, it was full dark and no one saw him mount the Major's horse and ride away into the night.

In the aftermath of the battle in which so many of Wellington's personal staff had died it was easy to report to a commander who did not know him personally. He was given leave to resign his commission and return to England and take over his estates.

★ ★ ★

When he presented himself to Blake and Sons they accepted that he was Richard Marshall and were pleased to hand over the sealed envelope they had held for so long. Inside Dickon discovered all the certificates and proofs that he needed and, thus armed, he visited the Rivenhall lawyers, Metcalf and Metcalf.

The older Mr. Metcalf greeted him with unbridled enthusiasm. 'My dear Lord Rivenhall, we have been searching for you for over eighteen months. We had begun to despair of finding you alive.'

Dickon shook the man's extended hand. 'I am pleased to be here, Mr. Metcalf. I am only sorry I did not realize you were looking for me sooner.'

'Sit down, my lord, and let us complete the formalities at once.' He paused and frowned. 'However I am sorry to have to inform you, my lord, but a senior clerk wrote to a certain William Rivenhall telling him that he is now the heir to the estate. Unfortunately this young man now believes that he is Lord Rivenhall and is at this very moment on his way to claim his inheritance.'

Dickon smiled thinly. 'A trifle embarrassing for both of us, Mr. Metcalf, but I am sure the young man will understand he is under a misapprehension.'

The elderly lawyer beamed. 'Good, I can leave you to sort this out?' The new Lord Rivenhall nodded. 'If you have need of any assistance in this matter please do not hesitate to send a messenger. I shall come directly.' They parted on good terms, both well satisfied by the meeting.

As his friend had predicted the lawyers had been happy to accept his claim, and so, armed with letters of introduction and the necessary documents, Dickon left London that afternoon and drove like a madman to Hampshire, determined to arrive before his rival.

*   *   *

Richard stopped talking. The silence hung heavy in the room. He finally raised his head and dared to meet the anguished eyes of the young woman he had come to love so dearly.

'Well, Millie, there you have it. I hated to lie to you, to everyone, but I had no choice, I made a vow to a dying man. I had to do my best to fulfil it. But I have failed in everything. I have failed Richard and I have failed you.'

Without moving consciously Amelia found herself kneeling at his feet. 'No, Richard, you have failed no-one. You can still succeed; I beg you, do not give up now.'

Damp-eyed he stared down at her, hardly able to believe his ears. 'Amelia, my love, can you not see, even if you do not expose me, in two days my colonel will be here and it will be over.'

'But it need not be. Do you love me, Richard?' Her outrageous question made him laugh in spite of his misery.

'What a question! Of course I do and I shall show you how much.' He scooped her on to his lap and Amelia received her first real kiss. When he finally placed her back on her feet she was adrift on a sea of pleasure. She had had no idea being a woman could be so wonderful.

'Then let us get married — now — today — by special licence. Then we can depart for an extended honeymoon and when Colonel Dewkesbury arrives we shall be gone. He will not wish to wait for our return and hopefully neither will William and his lawyers.'

Richard flushed. He had already considered that option and had obtained, some weeks ago, a special licence. However he had rejected it. He could not ask Amelia to risk everything for him; she deserved better.

She saw his distress at her suggestion

and it convinced her that she was right. 'Richard, we have no choice. If we do not, Rivenhall will go to William. And how long do you think the estate will survive with him at its head? He will ruin it. Do you think that Papa, Mama, Uncle Edward or Richard would want that?'

It was a masterstroke; a reason he could not push aside. He straightened, his vitality restored; once more in command of himself and the situation.

'Very well, my love, if you are sure then we will do it.' Smiling he dropped before her on one knee and clasped his hands to his chest in a theatrical manner. 'Miss Rivenhall, will you do me the great honor of becoming my wife?'

'Oh lah, your lordship, this is so sudden! You will have to speak to my guardian and I am afraid he is a tyrant and likely to refuse.' She had always loved playacting.

'For you I would do anything, my dear Miss Rivenhall,' Richard bleated, his voice an uncanny replica of the absent William. He surged upright and promptly asked himself permission to marry the young woman collapsed in hysterical giggles, in a most unseemly way, upon the sofa.

He reached down and pulled her, breathless, to her feet. Holding her at arm's length his expression sobered, but Amelia could feel his love surrounding her, holding her safe, whatever happened.

'My darling, listen to me. We shall be wed, but it will be a marriage in name only, do you understand what I mean?'

It was Amelia's turn to flush. 'Yes, I am not a child, Richard. But . . . ' she hesitated; even with their closeness she could not discuss a subject of such intimacy.

Richard took her almost roughly into his embrace. 'Little idiot! Listen to me. If things do not to go as planned and I lose the title then the marriage can be annulled. You will not be tied to a disgraced infantry captain.'

'It is you who are the idiot, Richard. Do you think I should care what others think of you? I love you, Lord Rivenhall or not. You told me you have sufficient funds to buy a small estate; then that is what we shall do if we lose Rivenhall.'

'And if I am clapped in jail, what then?'

For an instant Amelia's determination faltered. She shook her head. 'I do not care. I shall be a true wife or no wife at all.' She glared at the man she loved more than her heritage and her good name, daring him to disagree.

He reached over and tenderly pushed her hair from her flushed cheeks, held captive by her sparkling green eyes. He was lost. He could refuse his enchanting, courageous cousin nothing. 'I do not deserve you, my little love; and I know I should stand firm, but how can I? I love you too much to risk losing you. Let us be dammed to the consequences!'

Amelia laughed, aware that she would have to get used to his robust speech if she was to become his wife. She tilted her head to receive his gentle kiss then reluctantly he put her away from him.

'Enough, Millie, I pray that we have the rest of our lives for this. Go back to your bedchamber but be ready to leave for the church at nine sharp. Take Martha in the carriage with you. I shall meet you there.' Richard escorted his bride-to-be to the door, unlocked it, and Amelia slipped through.

She wanted to run and shout she was so full of joy, but instead returned to her room as stealthily as she had left it. She would keep her happiness contained until she was Lady Rivenhall, or Mrs. Jones; she really cared little which it turned out to be.

9

Amelia was too excited to sleep. She rekindled the oil lamps and all the candles and decided to begin sorting the garments she would need for her honeymoon. There would be little time for packing if they were to leave directly they returned from church.

Soon her bed, and the *chaise-longue*, cascaded with billows of material, a kaleidoscope of colour — silk, damask, dimity and muslin. Amelia had not realized how many gowns she had in her closet.

By dawn her enthusiasm for packing had wavered and she made herself a nest on the bed and fell asleep. It was there that Martha found her the next morning. She was so startled by the chaos that the breakfast tray almost joined the muddle of material on the floor.

'Miss Millie, whatever is all this?'

Amelia rubbed her eyes and surveyed the catastrophe of clothes she had caused. She stretched luxuriously and smiled radiantly at her bemused abigail. 'I was sorting my wardrobe for my honeymoon, Martha, and fell asleep.'

This time the tray did slip and with a deafening crash fell to the floor, scattering sweet rolls, butter pats and hot chocolate across the already overcrowded carpet. Martha's hands covered her face in consternation. She could see that at least two gowns had been soiled by her clumsiness.

Amelia scrambled out of bed, still smiling. 'Please do not look so worried, Martha dear, it does not matter. I should not have told you my news like that.'

'Oh, Miss Amelia, I am so sorry. It was such a shock!' Martha paused and saw that her young mistress was incandescent with happiness. Lady Rivenhall would have been pleased that her daughter had found love, and with such a man as Lord Rivenhall. 'When are you to be wed, Miss Millie?' She spoke as she stooped to collect the shards of broken pottery.

'This morning, by special licence, and you are to be my witness.'

'So soon?' This haste smacked of something clandestine and Martha's suspicions were raised.

'Yes, Martha. Why should we wait? I have no parent to consult, no friends to ask for advice, and Richard and I want to be together.'

Martha was unconvinced. Amelia needed her support for if Martha had an inkling of the real reason for the hasty ceremony she would try and stop it, send for Rivenhall, and all would be lost. Whatever Richard said, she knew, with certainty, that if he was exposed as an impostor and disgraced before the world he would never marry her. His pride would not allow it.

'Martha, listen to me. Lord Rivenhall and I are deeply in love and yesterday we kissed.' She heard Martha's hiss of disapproval. 'I know, we were very wrong, but Richard immediately proposed and,' she paused, blushing a little, 'we both knew it would no longer be possible for him to remain under the same roof as me, not unless we were man and wife.'

Martha's face creased in sympathetic smiles. 'Very right and proper, I'm sure. You did wrong, both of you, but are putting it right now, and I'm proud of you. Dear Lady Rivenhall would be pleased too, Miss Amelia.'

'I hope so, Martha. Now please help me bathe and dress, for we do not have long. The carriage will be outside in little over an hour and we still have to pack the trunks.'

Between them they made sense from the chaos and in good time the trunks were packed and waiting by the bedroom door. Amelia was dressed in a deep rose velvet walking dress, edged with cherry braid, and a matching pelisse; a pretty matching bonnet decorated with cherries completed the ensemble.

'You look a picture, Miss Millie. I wish your dear mama was here to see this day.'

Amelia nodded, and smiled mistily. She had no need to check her appearance in the mirror, she felt beautiful, from the top of her carefully coiffured hair to the tips of her cherry-red kid boots. She had the glow only brides can achieve.

Foster held open the door and the young footman handed them into the waiting carriage. John was on the box, the groom beside him. He had winked, in a most familiar way, when Amelia caught his eye. She smiled, as she settled back on the seat, happy her two favourite people were part of her secret.

The journey to Rivenhall Church was brief. The bridegroom was waiting outside with Peters and a rather nervous vicar, who thought the whole business distinctly odd, but did not wish to offend his new benefactor by asking awkward questions. Amelia thought Richard looked splendid in his regimentals, every inch a Lord.

'Good morning, Reverend Jeffries, thank you for helping Lord Rivenhall and I out of a dilemma.' The vicar nodded and smiled weakly. 'If we had had our banns read we would have offended so many local people, who believe such a celebration ought not to take place until a full year's mourning has been completed.'

Richard hid his smile; Amelia's explanation was ingenious. Amelia felt the vicar wavering and delivered the coup de grace. 'It was my mother's wish that we married. She did not think it proper for us to reside together unchaperoned any longer than was necessary.'

The vicar beamed. 'Absolutely, Miss Rivenhall, you have both behaved properly. When people hear you have fulfilled dear Lady Rivenhall's dying request, they will be happy for you both.'

Richard took Amelia's arm, Martha and Peters fell in behind them and the

Reverend Jeffries led the way. In less than twenty minutes Amelia emerged from the church a Rivenhall still, but now a Lady.

'I shall travel back with you, my love; Martha can return with Peters.' Richard handed his new wife into the waiting carriage and the groom shut the door and removed the steps, pushing them carefully into their allotted place, behind the coachman's seat.

Amelia glowed with happiness. Whatever Richard feared she believed nothing could separate them now. 'My darling Millie, you have made me the happiest of men. I pray you do not live to regret it.'

'Never, my love, never.' Richard drew her into his arms and she raised her head to receive his kiss. Lost in each other's arms they traveled the short distance back to Rivenhall.

No wedding breakfast was planned; they were to leave for their prolonged honeymoon on the continent immediately. They believed the trunks would be waiting by the front door ready to be loaded as soon as they returned. John was to drive the Rivenhall carriage and Martha and Peters were to follow behind in Richard's travelling chaise.

Lord and Lady Rivenhall arrived; blissfully unaware of the furore that awaited them. Foster had been told at the last minute of their wedding, and it had been his duty to inform the remainder of the staff. Unfortunately William had returned to Rivenhall as Foster was making a grand announcement to the staff assembled in the hall. If he had, as expected, spread the word discreetly, all might still have been well. Now it was too late, the secret was revealed. William was not so easily deceived as the Vicar.

He had his valet and the lawyers remove the trunks. Then he waited to greet the happy couple. Hardly allowing them time to gain their feet, he pounced.

'Married are you? Well, much good will it do you, Cousin Amelia, for by this evening your husband will be in custody, exposed as an impostor and thief, and you will be the abandoned wife of a felon.'

Amelia was glad of Richard's arm around her waist. The venom in William's voice made her shiver. Richard said nothing, he was too angry to trust himself. Instead he ignored his accuser, brushed past him as if he was invisible. He calmly led Amelia in to Rivenhall; no one would have known that all was not well, or that their lives were about to be ruined.

William, losing all sense in his eagerness to follow the hated couple, shoved Martha out of his path; her cry of distress as she stumbled backwards down the steps made the newlyweds turn back.

Amelia ran down to kneel beside her injured maid. 'How could you do that, you brute? You have caused injury to someone who has never done you harm.'

Richard swung round, his fists clenched.

Nobody harmed a member of the fairer sex and escaped unscathed when he was present. But William, knowing he was facing punishment of the most parlous kind, shot inside, finding refuge from Richard's fury, with his lawyers, in the drawing-room. Richard, his quarry flown, leapt back down the stairs, to lift Martha, moaning quietly, in his arms.

'It is my ankle, my lord, I think it is broke. Oh, I am so sorry, how will you manage now, madam?' Even in her pain she had remembered to address Amelia correctly.

'You must not worry, Martha, we are no longer going away. Annie can take care of my needs until you recover.' She moved to Richard's side. 'Will you take Martha to her room, and I will send John for the doctor.' In the confusion following the accident they had temporarily forgotten William's threats.

Martha was made comfortable, her ankle splinted and a maid assigned to take care of her every need. Satisfied she had done all she could Amelia hurried back to join her husband in the library, in sombre mood, her earlier elation vanished like the early-morning mist that had followed them to church.

Richard was staring morosely into the fire; there was no sign of his earlier bravado. 'Richard, all is not yet lost, you must not despair.'

He kicked a log, sending a shower of sparks up the chimney. 'We cannot leave now; William has made sure of that. We are trapped here and there is nothing we can do. Colonel Dewkesbury is expected tomorrow or maybe even tonight, and then we shall be undone.' He walked over to his wife and drew her to him in a tender embrace. 'I have no excuse, my darling; I have ruined your life, for that I shall never forgive myself.'

'You have ruined nothing, my love. It is William who was done that. I have never liked the man but now I positively loathe him. He is a despicable toad to attack poor Martha like that.'

Richard's lips compressed at the

reminder. 'If he comes within arm's reach without those black crows of lawyers for protection he will not survive the encounter, that I promise you.' To his astonishment a peal of bubbling laughter greeted this pronouncement.

'Richard, you are being ridiculous, honorable and brave, but still ridiculous.'

This contradictory statement had him flummoxed but it lightened his mood and made him smile, which had been Amelia's intention.

'You can hardly murder a relative, however obnoxious he has been, and especially not within these walls. Then you really would be a candidate for prison.'

'You are, of course, my dear, perfectly correct. It would not do to confuse the runners; they will be here to arrest me for fraud and deception, not murder.'

'You shall not be arrested for anything. I truly believe God will not let such an evil man take the reins of

Rivenhall. A solution will present itself, you must have faith, Richard.'

Richard shifted uncomfortably. He paid lip service to religion but, like most soldiers, had little real belief in the innate goodness of man, or the benign intervention of a supreme power. He had seen too many atrocities committed and then justified by war.

But looking down into Amelia's lovely, earnest face and seeing such conviction in her eyes he was nearly convinced of the power of good over evil. 'If it pleases you, my love, I shall try and believe, but I rather think you have enough faith for the two of us. You know I would give you anything that it is in my power to give. Maybe your God will feel as I do and grant your wish?'

Amelia stretched up and kissed his cheek. 'Oh, Richard, you shall see; and he is not my God, he is yours as well; he is everyone's who cares to listen to his voice.'

'I pray you are right, Millie.'

'There, you see, deep inside you, you do believe,' Amelia teased him, smiling.

Richard tousled her hair and strode to the window. 'It is a glorious day, shall we go for a ride? If I do not keep busy I know I shall go in search of Rivenhall and relieve my frustrations on him.'

'Richard, you must not.' Then she saw his grin. 'You wretch! You should not joke about such things, and yes I would love to ride.'

Amelia returned to her own bed chamber, Richard went to his. It did not seem appropriate to make changes in their sleeping arrangements as matters stood. She had sent a message to John and their mounts were saddled and waiting when they arrived a short time later, but it was not Prince and Sultan who stamped impatiently, but Dolly and Sultan.

'What the devil is going on here, John, is this some kind of prank?' Lord Rivenhall was not pleased.

'Do not rail at John, please, it was my doing, Richard. I think it is time you tried Sultan again. He likes you; look how he is rubbing his head against your arm.'

Richard scratched the enormous chestnut muzzle then turned and, without further discussion, swung into the saddle, gathering up the reins as he did so. Amelia held her breath but Sultan merely shook his head, jangling his bit and stamping his hooves again, eager to get out and stretch his legs.

John hastily threw Amelia onto the pretty dappled mare and both riders and horses, in perfect harmony, clattered out under the arch, to enjoy an exhilarating, and uneventful, ride.

★   ★   ★

William watched them go and his lips curled with hate. They would pay for humiliating him. When the Colonel arrived he would make sure he knew the full story, make sure the proud Miss Rivenhall was knocked down from her lofty perch. Before the day was out he would be master here and she needn't think she would receive any favors from him.

*   *   *

Amelia spent an inordinate time at her ablutions wishing to fill the dreary space until it was time to change for dinner. Richard had changed out of his uniform and taken himself off to the estate office, insisting it was better if they remained apart, in the circumstances. Amelia feared he was going to insist on an annulment and have their union put aside.

With breaking heart and heavy eyes she saw the colonel's carriage bowling down the drive. She looked at the clock on the mantle-shelf. The time would be forever etched upon her memory. She knew her life was going to be irrevocably changed by the arrival of the man who had come to denounce her husband.

10

The colonel was not alone. Two rather uncouth, plainly dressed men emerged from the carriage behind him. Amelia noted that the men had a military bearing. Why had Dewkesbury brought two ex-soldiers with him?

Then she knew! She felt faint. She ran to the door, praying that a direct appeal from her might avoid the calamity. The men were Bow Street Runners; there could be no other explanation. The decision had already been made; the colonel had come to arrest Richard.

She flew down the stairs, oblivious to Foster's stare of disapproval, and slid to a halt in front of the man her husband, and her departed cousin, had honored and respected above all others, apart from the Duke himself.

If Lord Dewkesbury was in any way

put out by her undignified arrival he was too much the gentleman to show it. He bowed; his cropped grey hair matched his penetrating grey eyes. 'Good afternoon, Miss Rivenhall, I hope my early arrival does not incommode you?'

* * *

Amelia curtsied. 'No, my Lord, Richard and I are delighted you are here. Foster, have Lord Dewkesbury's bags conveyed to the green room.' She hesitated, eyeing the two silent men standing by the door. 'Will your, err . . . friends, be staying also, my Lord?'

Dewkesbury's expression was puzzled, then he smiled, no longer looking so forbidding. 'Good heavens, my dear, these two good men take care of me, they will find their own accommodations.' The relief on Amelia's face was noted by the colonel. Swallowing hard she attempted to smile, but made a sorry job of it. 'Shall we go somewhere more comfortable, my dear? This is not the place for a cozy conversation.'

'Yes, my lord, of course,' Amelia stammered, 'the library is my favourite room.'

'Then to the library we shall go.' He threaded Amelia's unresisting arm through his, and, still in his outdoor clothes, allowed her to lead him to the room away from prying eyes and listening years.

Inside he guided her to the chesterfield and gently seated her. He hated to see a beautiful lady in distress. He removed his cape and threw it casually across the back of a chair, before seating himself beside her on the sofa.

'Now, my dear, I think you must tell me all.'

'Richard and I were married this morning; he did not want to, but I insisted. I love him, my lord, and he is a brave, good and honest man. William Rivenhall, who sent for you, is a despicable coward, he is a profligate gambler, a drunkard, and he pushed my maid, Martha, downstairs this morning and she broke her ankle in the tumble.'

The colonel's eyes glittered. 'And where is this person now?'

'He is hiding from Richard.'

He chuckled. 'I am surprised he still breathes. For a moment I feared Richard had already disposed of him.'

Amelia smiled wanly. She liked this tall, spare man and wished that they had not met under such invidious circumstances. 'Richard is working in the estate office, my lord, I shall fetch him.' Then she remembered her lack of manners. 'I am sorry, would you like refreshments?'

'No, thank you. I shall get this business settled first.' The words were harsh but his tone was not unkind. They both rose and she politely curtsied. He led the way to the door and opened it.

William had been loitering in the corridor and seized his chance. He rushed forward, furious Amelia had had the opportunity to converse with Lord Dewkesbury before him. Amelia ignored him and swept past, head high, determined not to show their enemy that she was crumbling inside with terror and misery.

William grabbed her arm, restraining her. Victory was so nearly his; he had no need to pretend any more. 'It is over, cousin. You shall not be so high and mighty now. Your husband will be thrown in jail and do not think that I shall allow you to continue to live here, sullying the Rivenhall name. I shall see that you are destitute and forced to find a menial position, and your wretched family servants with you.'

An iron hand took William's and removed it from Amelia's arm. In a voice that had frequently reduced battle-hardened soldiers to trembling terror the colonel spoke.

'You are not a gentleman, Rivenhall. If you dare to lay another finger on Lady Rivenhall I will break your neck. Do I make myself clear? Now disappear — vanish from my sight.'

William shrivelled and slunk back

down the corridor like a whipped cur. Let them all abuse him if they wished, his moment of triumph was coming and he would have his revenge.

* * *

Richard had heard the carriage and was waiting for the knock to summon him. He had failed his dearest friend and even worse, he had failed the woman he loved more than life itself. There had never been the time, or the desire, for lengthy entanglements and he had always viewed romantic attachment with disgust. Love was for dandified gentleman, not for men of action. Then all had changed when he had met Amelia. The incomprehensible became as clear as day. He had derided others who declared they would die for their love. But now he knew that he would, in one instant, trade his own existence to protect his wife.

It wasn't Foster who came in. His courage almost deserted him when he saw the abject desolation reflected on Amelia's face. For the last time he held her close, pressed against the heart that beat solely for her.

He could feel the wet of her tears leaking through his shirt and he wanted to roar his frustration, to draw his sword and slay those who had brought her to this state. But neither William Rivenhall, despicable though he was, nor his ex-colonel was to blame. He had caused this and felt his heart contract with sadness and his eyes fill with tears of shame.

Gently he tipped her lovely ashen face and placed a tender farewell kiss upon her lips. 'Remember, my darling, whatever happens, I love you and you must be brave.'

Amelia rubbed her face on his shirt, thus completing the ruin of his starched cravat, and sniffed inelegantly. 'I like your colonel, Richard. Maybe he will let us leave, slip away before the Runners come; he does not look like a cruel man.'

'No, he is not cruel, but he is a man of honour. He must do his duty, I would expect nothing else.' With his thumbs he tenderly removed the tear-streaks from her face and straightened, once more in full control. Whatever happened he could endure it, as long as his darling Millie was kept safe and did not have to suffer for his folly.

United they walked back through the maze of corridors and into the main passageway and down to the small drawing-room where Colonel, Dewkesbury waited. Amelia felt like a French aristocrat walking to the guillotine, for if Richard was to be taken from her she might as well be dead. Life would have no meaning without him.

They heard the sound of urgent voices through the door but could not recognize the speaker or the words. Richard halted and for a brief, poignant moment, held Amelia to him, breathing in her familiar perfume, for what, he knew, would be the last time.

Too wretched to speak they kissed

and Richard then disentangled himself from Amelia's desperate, clinging arms and stepped away. He could not meet her eyes. His bearing was rigid, his military background giving him the courage to stride to his fate.

Amelia walked behind him, head up, trying to be as brave as he. She dared a glance around the room. The hateful William, and his legal team gathered like vultures waiting for the kill, hid in the window embrasure, as far away as possible from the colonel and his retainers.

Richard halted two paces from his commanding officer and saluted smartly; the colonel returned his gesture. If the situation had not been so serious Amelia would have smiled at the sight of two men, out of uniform, saluting each other.

'Well, Richard, what is all this about, my boy? It seems I have been fetched on a wild goose chase.' To everyone's incredulity the colonel stepped forward and enveloped the man standing in front of him in a bear hug. 'I must congratulate you, dear boy, on having the good sense to marry such an enchanting young lady; and also coming into the title, and inheriting Rivenhall. I am certain you will make an excellent fist of it.'

If Dewkesbury had not been holding him Richard might have fallen. The colonel knew he was an impostor but had just acknowledged him publically as Lord Rivenhall. The one outcome they had not considered.

He found his voice. 'Thank you, sir; I am indeed a fortunate man.' That he was not referring to his marriage was clear to at least three others in the room.

'Indeed you are, Richard, indeed you are,' his saviour replied dryly. 'Now, my boy, take care of your wife, she seems a little unwell.'

Richard spun and caught Amelia just as she collapsed in a swoon. With his beloved in his arms he grinned at Dewkesbury, his joy plain to see.

'Take Lady Rivenhall to her rooms,

Richard, then when she is settled come back; there are matters we must discuss.'

'Yes, sir, I shall be down directly.'

As Richard left the room carrying his precious burden, the colonel, flanked by his men, marched briskly to confront the cowering trio, trying to disappear behind the heavy brocade curtains.

'Rivenhall, you have caused enough damage by your damned impertinence. I suggest you remove yourself, and these persons, from this house, before more harm is done.'

William, who had been certain he was right, now perceived that by his appalling error of judgment, he had made himself a pair of implacable enemies. It was fortunate that he had not been in a position to view the expression of relief and joy on Richard's face when he was acknowledged as Lord Rivenhall or he might have reconsidered his position.

'I must most humbly apologize for my mistake. It is to be hoped that Lord

Rivenhall,' (to call Richard *Lord* almost choked him), 'will understand how this unfortunate circumstance arose. He is a fair and honest man.'

'If you are suggesting Lord Rivenhall will not pursue the matter I should not be too sanguine. There is the matter of your intemperate treatment of Lady Rivenhall.'

William blanched. If Lord Dewkesbury told Richard that he had manhandled his precious wife then his miserable existence would be over. He bowed; terrified he would not be away before retribution struck. He didn't wait to collect his belongings; his valet could follow with them. He fled, trailing his legal crows behind him, squawking loudly about payment for their efforts on his behalf.

Lord Dewkesbury smiled. He had enjoyed routing young Dickon's enemies. Captain Jones was a hero and deserved the spoils of war. He chuckled to himself. 'Stand easy, lads. You will not be needed now.'

'Yes, sir.' The ex-soldiers relaxed their aggressive stance. 'We will take care of your baggage and then find ourselves lodging. Are we staying long at Rivenhall, my Lord?'

'A day or two, no longer. I can hear Lord Rivenhall returning. I shall call you if I need you.'

'Yes, sir,' they replied again and exited smartly, bowing politely to the gentleman they mistakenly remembered as being Captain Jones.

Richard grinned and shook each by the hand. 'Good to see you both. Peters will direct you to your rooms. Just ask if you require anything further.' Still smiling Lord Rivenhall joined Lord Dewkesbury in the drawing-room.

'Richard, how is your wife?'

'Fully recovered, thank you, sir. She will be with us directly. Millie is not given to fainting fits, I assure you, but the worry of the past few weeks has taken its toll.'

'I am sure it has. Sit down, young man, I wish you to explain to me why I find Captain Richard Jones masquerading as Major Richard Marshall.'

When the long story was told the colonel shook his head. For an awful instant Richard thought his commanding officer had changed his mind.

'You had no choice, my boy; I would have done the same myself. Rivenhall is in better hands, by far, than it would have been with William Rivenhall. I disliked the man on sight. I can tell a rogue when I see one.'

'But what if he had been a different sort of person, would you have held for me then, my Lord?'

Dewkesbury yawned and stretched his legs, frowning at the dust marring the shine on his Hessians. 'If Rivenhall had been a decent fellow I doubt all this would have been necessary.' He looked up then rose smoothly to his feet. 'Lady Rivenhall, my dear, I am delighted to see you well again.'

Amelia, ignoring her husband, flew across the room and flung her arms around the colonel. 'Thank you, my lord, thank you. I knew my prayers would be answered in some fashion, but never dreamt that you would support Richard's claim like this.'

Colonel Dewkesbury, unused to close contact with a female person, patted Amelia awkwardly on the back, his face a study of embarrassment. He cleared his throat. 'Well, well, my dear, yes, umm . . . what . . . '

Richard, laughing openly, rescued his beleaguered friend. He encircled her waist and lifted her, spinning her round to place her, firmly, on a nearby sofa. Before she could protest at such rough treatment, he leant down and dropped a kiss on her open mouth.

'Excellent,' Dewkesbury said, having placed himself out of harm's way on the chair at the far side of the room. 'You always had quick reactions.'

Amelia turned her burning cheeks and hid them on Richard's shoulder. Too late she saw that her gratitude had been expressed in a way that had embarrassed their guest and amused her husband.

'Now, I have some sound advice for

both of you.' At his serious tone they both looked up, paying full attention. 'Once Rivenhall has recovered from his fright he is going to wish to cause you as much grief as he can contrive. There are several hundred men and women in England, and on the continent, that could support his story. You were too well known to go unrecognized. The similarity of your appearance is remarkable but no one who fought alongside you would ever mistake you for Richard Marshall.'

'What do you suggest, my lord? Shall we go as planned on our extended honeymoon?'

'Exactly, my boy. Absent yourselves from England for several months. By then anyone Rivenhall may have contacted will no longer be interested. It will be stale news.'

'We cannot leave without Martha, Richard. She would be devastated.'

Richard frowned. 'We have to leave immediately, my love, we cannot risk William returning with new witnesses.'

'You have no choice, my dear Lady Rivenhall. I am sure your maid will understand the urgency.'

'No, my lord, she will not. She is not privy to our secret.'

'Of course she is not. Well, you will have to think of a convincing reason, because I fear you have no choice.' When Colonel Dewkesbury spoke with such authority Amelia knew she had to comply. Richard's safety was paramount; Martha would have to be left behind.

Richard squeezed her hand sympathetically. 'We have more than we ever dreamed, my love, we cannot expect to have it all.' Amelia sighed, her husband, as usual, was correct. She would have to take Annie as her dresser, instead.

'There is one other thing, Richard. Visiting London, or even Bath, in season will be too risky.'

'I have no desire to frequent the overheated ballrooms of the *ton*. I would rather have my teeth pulled.'

Amelia nodded. 'Then I shall visit on

my own. I never attended a ball, or mixed with the *ton*. We have a house in London, which my parents used, before mama's health failed. I shall open it when we return.'

Richard glared down at his wife. 'You will do no such thing, Amelia. I shall not allow you to . . . ' his voice faltered as the room filled with the chuckles of both Lord Dewkesbury and his wife. Ruefully he acknowledged he had been roundly teased, again.

His wife smiled up at him, her eyes large with love. 'I am so happy; it is going to be such fun being married to you Richard.'

They did not hear the door close quietly behind Lord Dewkesbury as he left them alone, for the first time since their marriage, to celebrate their love.